The Book of Lost Magic

The Book of Lost Magic

A JAMS Tale

NEW Reads Publications | Jacksonville, FL

Published in the United States by NEW Reads Publications. NEW Reads Publications is a registered trademark of NEW Reads Publications, LLC in Jacksonville, FL.

newreadspub.com

ISBN 978-1-7357219-6-5 (hardback)
ISBN 978-1-7357219-7-2 (ebook)

Printed in the United States of America

Interior design by Nikesha Elise Williams
Cover design by Erin Kendrick of Erin is Creative

First Edition: September 2022

For the legacy of Augusta Savage and the youth of Duval county—past, present and future—may you dream bigger than the world in which you reside.

CHAPTER 1

The Cummer Museum of Art & Gardens

The sky was warm and sunny as the class walked into the Cummer Museum of Art and Gardens in Jacksonville, Florida. A complete 360 from how the day would soon turn out. From this class, one girl stood out from the rest. Her name was Mira, and she had an immensely strong personality with looks that didn't fit what society called the typical body of a twelve-year-old girl.

Mira's strong personality, defensiveness, and her general treatment of others caused her to get into a fight with a fellow classmate while they toured the Olmsted Garden.

"No one ever understands what I'm going through. All you had to do was listen to me. Ugh," Mira yelled.

This fight was not as serious as it seemed. Mira's sullen attitude was due to the fact she couldn't have control over where the class went to explore in the garden first.

"Ester is always trying to control everything," Mira mutters to herself, continuing the argument on her own. "Why does everything have to go her way?"

Mira really wanted the class and her teachers to feel bad for her. She wanted them to feel guilty and change their minds about what they would explore first.

Unfortunately, she hadn't calculated all the potential possibilities and outcomes. One, they could have just ignored her. Two, they could have changed the location and gone to where she wanted to go, which was what Mira was hoping for. But the last outcome, the real outcome, was completely different.

Mira's classmate Ester snapped at her, "You think you are the only person in this class and every decision has to be made around what Mira wants and not what most of the class wants. You need to learn a serious lesson because your personality will get you in trouble one day."

"You're just mad that your personality is the only thing people like about you because you're ugly." Mira often spoke without thinking about how her words affected others.

She wandered off alone away from the group into the Italian Garden, despite the teacher's orders, causing a scene as she left. Mira kicked up dirt and trampled on the flower beds as her teachers called her name and demanded that she turn around, but she refused to listen.

As Mira walked the Italian Garden, she paced around the fountain ringed in tall shrubbery. Doing laps helped her calm down. She also noticed the atmosphere was different from when she was with her classmates. The bright, sunny day had become darker and frightening, and it was almost hard to breathe.

"Mira, Mira, Mira!" her teachers and classmates yelled. "Where are you?" they called.

Mira heard the voices of the teachers and students looking for her, but she kept walking through the garden, which somehow turned into a dense forest. Even though she was scared, she kept walking, feeling too guilty and embarrassed to go back because of the scene she had caused. Mira couldn't accept being wrong.

She stopped underneath the large Cummer tree. The old oak with its long limbs and massive trunk kept her shaded and hidden as she stared at her reflection in the dark, clear water. So calm and entranced by her own reflection in the water, Mira lost her balance on one of the tree's roots and began to tumble forward. The dark bottom of the reflecting pool began to glow with an intense burning blue light as Mira fell inside. By the time the rest of her class and her teachers got into the garden where she was, she had vanished.

CHAPTER 2

Aeolus, the Kingdom in the Sky

The brash sound of trumpets blew throughout the kingdom filled with wealth and nobility. Golden architecture surrounded everything as far as the eye could see. An assembly of people cheered as the kingdom's army brigade marched carrying the banner flag with the royal family's crest on it. It was a large star with two intertwining lines that met in the middle. With every single wave of the flag, more cheers and applause came from the adoring crowd. Looking from a large watchtower were the prince and princess of Aeolus, the Kingdom in the Sky.

Their names were Kai and Kam. Kai was the cocky and smug prince of the kingdom. Kam was the young but wise-beyond-her-years princess of Aeolus. Their physical appearances gave away the fact that these two siblings were twins. Their grayish-white dreadlocks in matching high ponytails blew as the wind entered the watchtower. A muscular jester paraded along with the army brigade, clutching a salpinx and wearing a hat with white and gold stripes across it. As he marched, he lifted his horn from his side. "Ladies and gentlemen, give it up for your charming, brave, dazzling, and oh-so divine prince and princess of Aeolus. Kai and Kam!"

Kai's body boosted from the watchtower as he performed aerial acrobatics. He ended the show by slamming his fist into the ground. The ground below him crumbled from the impact, as if the foundation was weak. Kam leapt from the watchtower, floating elegantly like an angel down toward the crater her brother had created.

"Can you at least act like you have some sort of common sense?!" she asked through bared teeth.

"Well, excussssse me, princess." Kai grinned at his clearly aggravated sister.

The jester cleared his throat as he spoke to the crowd. "Alright everyone. Now it's time for the best part. The prince and princess will be setting off to a new world! What mysterious creatures will the twins come across?" The crowd was left in suspense as he turned away from them and toward the twins. "So, which one of you will do the honors and open the portal?"

Kai eagerly raised his hand with confidence. "I'll do it," he said. "We don't want Miss Pretty princess to burn through her magic again." He sneered at his sister.

Kam paid her brother's sly comment no mind. Kai hopped off of the cracked concrete and squatted on the ground; he slammed his fist into it, activating his magical powers. A small summoning circle arose from the ground. The blue light coming from the newly opened portal engulfed the entire kingdom.

Kai, full of pride in his abilities, excitedly ran toward the portal entrance. But before he could get even a foot in, Kam grabbed him by the collar of his shirt.

"You know you're forgetting our weapons, right?" she yelled as she yanked him back.

"Oh yeah…oops," he said, embarrassed by his excitement.

Two soldiers walked toward the twins. In the middle of the soldiers was an elderly man. He wore a white robe with gold accents around the sleeves. In his hands, he carried a large chest that he struggled to hold up. The old man stopped in front of the twins and dropped the chest. "Your weapons, my prince and princess," he huffed between wheezing breaths.

Kam opened the chest. Inside of it were two weapons: a two-edged sword with a golden handle and a bow and arrow with a fully stocked quiver. Kai grabbed the sword and put it in a sheath on his back. Kam grabbed the bow and quiver of arrows and secured it with a strap that wrapped around her chest.

Finally, we can get out of this place, Kam thought to herself. I'm tired of looking at the same thing and hearing the same voices every day.

Kai looked at his sister and smirked. He could read her mind and knew all of her thoughts. As they walked into the portal, the elderly man said to them, "Remember: your patches will guide you back home," but by then, the twins had already left, prepared for their new journey.

CHAPTER 3

Pollutio

The world was quiet, desolate, as if the whole place was a library. There was no person in sight in this world that held Earth's waste like a jail. Everyone was hidden in their little houses made of rubble and trash. It was quiet, almost too quiet to hold any living thing that was capable of making a sound. Only for a boy whose aura made sound alone, along with his sharp personality… Bash.

Bash had been living alone since the age of 11 when his mother and father were taken away from him. It left him with no choice but to depend on himself. He went around helping others in hopes they would, in return, offer him something to help him stay alive.

"OH! You're back, son," stated an old man greeting Bash with a smile from ear to ear.

"Yep, I came to see if I could help you with anything," Bash replied.

He hoped the man would have a job for him so he could get some food or some change to get something to eat. The man looked around for a minute, wondering if he had something for Bash to do. Even though Bash had been alone from a young age, he still had the old man that watched over him. The elder taught him one important lesson. The world didn't owe him a thing, so everything he wanted he had to work hard for.

"I do have one job if you are interested. There is one thing, though: this job requires you to go past the trash city into the desert of scraps. When you arrive, look for a sparkly red gem," stated the old man.

"Why do you need a sparkly red gem, if you don't mind me asking, sir?" Bash asked with one eyebrow raised higher than the other.

"Oh, it's just something personal to me that I would like to keep to myself, son," the old man said, turning his big smile upside down to the ground.

"Okay. That's fine. Challenge accepted," Bash said happily, trying to change the old man's mind from whatever he was thinking about.

Bash hurried to his small hut and prepared for the journey to the desert of scraps. The journey would last for three days and two nights, so he would need some things for sleeping and to help him keep warm. The old man gave Bash a map and a staff that had spikes sticking out of the top like a porcupine for his protection. The map had a mark on it to show where the red gem should be located. After getting all his supplies, he began his journey.

I have to make sure I bring back this gem. Maybe I can make the old man proud enough to give me food whenever I need it. When I come back with that red beauty, that old man is not going to believe that I did it all alone. He will want me to be his helper for the rest of his life, Bash pondered, looking forward to his life after coming back with the gem.

He walked for what he believed to be hours. It was getting dark. Engrossed in his daydream, he was finally woken by weird noises behind him. Curious, Bash turned around to see two kids following behind him. A boy and a girl he recognized from his village. They were twins around the age of 10.

"Hey," Bash smiled. "What are you two doing here? You know your parents will be worried, right? You have to go back, even though I would love to have you two join me," Bash said happily to the pair.

The two looked at each other, then to Bash. "Aww man, we wanted to join you on your journey. The old man made it sound so fun." The boy pouted.

"Please, can we join you?" the twins asked at the same time.

"I'm sorry, but you can't come with me. It's too dangerous. I don't want anything bad to happen to you two. You both are like family. Do you guys know the way back?"

The twins shook their heads up and down in unison.

"Okay, well, off you go, and tell your mom and dad I said hi." Bash sent the twins off and continued on his journey. He walked until daybreak and finally made it to his mark. Now all he had to do was look around for the red gem. Searching and searching, Bash saw a bright color, but it wasn't red. The sapphire-colored light source appeared in the sky and it was growing bigger like a stain on a paper towel. Bash was surprised at the sight of another set of twins falling through a bright blue hole. Being careful, Bash hid behind a hill of trash to make sure they were not a threat. Suddenly, right after the twins, he saw a girl fall through a second blue hole in the sky.

"Well, this is interesting." In shock but not forgetting his main purpose, Bash continued on his own, but he couldn't help but be drawn to the new people. Where had they come from? Why were they here?

CHAPTER 4

Falling through the blue light of the portal from Aeolus, Kai and Kam could not see where they were going. The portal opening from their kingdom in the sky had closed. They were cut off from home and unsure of where they were going or where they had ended up.

"Where are we?" Kam asked. "This doesn't look like the realm we are supposed to be in."

The place was full of trash and looked very sketchy and not appealing to the eye. The twins hesitantly took in the new and different world. Curious, they walked around to explore. As they did, they saw a girl, Mira, fall from another portal with the same blue light into the new and strange world. Mira landed face-down in the dirt like a kid falling from a bike. But Kai and Kam didn't notice. They didn't see her fall. They were too focused on the portal. They wanted to leave, so they made a run for the blue light, hoping it would help them get back home.

"No, no, it's closing!" the twins screamed in unison.

On the ground, Mira started to stir. Once on her feet she looked at the twins as if they had committed a murder.

"Yeah, I'm definitely okay. Thanks for checking on me," she said.

Kai and Kam looked from each other to the girl and back. Mira was also confused. As a human from Earth she had no idea about the supernatural, gods, portals, and the magic Kai and Kam had grown up with.

"This is so crazy, but so cool," Mira said in awe. "So I'll forget about you two not helping me."

Kai and Kam looked at Mira curiously. They shrugged their shoulders as the tension quickly lifted as they introduced themselves to one another.

Kai extended his hand and said, "Hi, I'm Kai, and this is my twin sister, Kam."

Mira shook Kai's hand as she said, "Hi, I'm Mira. Where are you from?"

"We are the royal heirs to the kingdom of Aeolus. I am Princess Kam."

"Oh," Mira said, looking down at the ground. "I'm from America on Earth. We don't have any royals there."

Consumed with feelings of insecurity, Mira didn't overreact like she usually would when meeting someone new. Instead of trying to make herself the center of attention and ostracizing herself away from Kai and Kam, she decided to try and get along with the twins. The three of them figured that, since the world was foreign to them, it would be fun for them to go exploring. Mira led the way into the new world. Kai and Kam, just a step behind her, looked at each other with intensity, like they wanted to burn a hole through the other.

"They aren't working, Kam," said Kai.

"What isn't working?" Mira asked curiously.

"Oh, at home we have powers, but ever since we've been here, they don't seem to be working," Kai said.

"I think it has something to do with this realm," Kam added. "But every other realm we've been to, our powers have worked."

Mira's eyes lit up like a Christmas tree when Kai and Kam mentioned their powers.

"This is so cool," Mira squealed excitedly. "Earth is so boring."

The twins laughed at Mira's happiness upon discovering they had powers. They considered her odd to have never experienced the supernatural. What is Earth like? they wondered. Before they could think about it too long, Mira broke into their thoughts.

"Okay, what are we waiting for?" she interrupted. "Let's go exploring."

Mira jumped like a child opening a gift as she continued to lead the way in the new world. Kai and Kam followed behind, trying and failing to tap into the power on the fritz inside of them.

CHAPTER 5

Kai said, "Wow, this place is cool."

The area where Kai, Kam, and Mira stood was shaped like a world made of Lego bricks because of how compact all the trash was. The world was so isolated that on their journey to the city, they didn't see a single person until they finally made it.

There, they saw a boy and a girl who walked past them with smiles that seemed drawn on.

"Hey, you guys from around here?" the girl asked.

"N——…"

Before Mira could finish her sentence, the twins pulled her away from the pair.

"Don't you know not to talk to strangers? They will never have good intentions," the twins said in unison.

"You guys are too serious," Mira said. "It is also rude in my world to ignore people when they speak." She laughed away the twins' cautiousness and walked toward the boy and girl..

"Sorry, guys. No, we are not from here," Mira said. "We are kind of lost and don't know where we are going."

"Oh really… that's cool," the boy said weirdly. "Why don't you guys come along with us, and we can take you somewhere really cool," the boy said after an uncomfortable pause.

Kam tried to decline. "I think we are fine, but thanks."

"Come on, don't you want to have some fun?" Mira asked, jokingly. "I don't think anything bad will happen. Let's just go."

The twins did not want to go with this pair of strangers because they didn't trust people easily. Then again, they also didn't want to ruin the moment. Begrudgingly, they agreed with Mira and decided to follow behind the strange boy and girl who had foreign markings all over their faces.

"Just a little further," said the girl.

The five of them walked for about an hour at least until they arrived at a cave. Even though the sun was setting Mira, Kai, and Kam followed the pair like three baby ducks waddling behind the first thing they saw. Suddenly, the boy and girl stopped in the middle of the dark cave.

"Hey, guys, we are going to have to stop here," the boy said, turning around and abruptly halting his march deep into the cave. "Let's cut to the chase—we really don't care about you having fun. All we want are your things."

Mira, Kai, and Kam looked at each other, confused. Mira was the most confused and hurt. Her face flushed with embarrassment as she realized she should have listened to the twins.

"That's not going to happen," Kai said.

He reached for his sword on his back only to realize it was not there.

"My sword is gone!" Kai roared through the cave.

"Looking for this?" The boy brandished Kai's sword. "You should really be more careful about who you follow."

"How did you? When did you?" Kai asked, trying to figure out when his sword was stolen.

"Yeah. Come on, give me yours! NOW!" the girl demanded of Kam as she stepped behind the boy holding Kai's sword.

Kam took off her bow and arrows and threw them at the girl then backed up with Mira and Kai until they felt an arm around them. Another stranger was behind them. A boy. They immediately jumped away from him, thinking that he was with the pair trying to rob them of their belongings. But he held on to them to reassure them that he could be trusted.

The new stranger said, "Give it back or you'll have to deal with me."

Recognition alighted in the boy and girl's faces as they looked at the stranger who had stepped out to protect them. They threw Kai's sword and Kam's bow and arrows back at them and scampered away.

"Get your stuff," the stranger said.

Kai and Kam reached for their weapons and secured them once again on their backs, never taking their eyes away from the strange boy who'd saved them. Mira waited silently, not knowing who to trust, who to follow, or where to go.

The stranger said, "Guys, come with me. I'll protect you and guide you. I know it might be hard to trust someone else with what's going on, but just follow me."

Desperate, Mira, Kai, and Kam had no choice but to follow behind the new stranger. As they did, he turned to the conniving couple and said, "You can forget about taking their things. They're with me."

The would-be thieves looked at the boy in fear and ran out of the cave.

"Thank you for saving us, but why did you do it?" Kai asked.

"And how do we know we can trust you?" Kam asked.

"First, I will introduce myself," the strange boy said. "My name is Bash, and as you can see, this realm is not your normal realm because it's full of trash, which probably in your realm is seen as abnormal. I've heard of people like you coming to Pollutio before."

"You know who we are?" Kai and Kam asked in unison.

"Why would he know who you are?" Mira asked, with attitude.

Bash rolled his eyes and continued explaining the rules and ways of Pollutio. "In this world, your shiny and new things have no value. The only reason those people wanted to steal your stuff is because, in this realm, stealing is an everyday occurrence. It is our way of life."

"Seems like a crappy way of life to me," Mira muttered.

"Just let him finish explaining," Kam snapped, confronting Mira.

"Thank you," Bash said. "I just want you to know that I don't want your things, and you should know it's going to be hard for you guys to survive alone, so let me help you."

"Why do you want to help us?" Kai asked, eyeing Bash suspiciously.

Mira, Kai, and Kam stared from each other to Bash and back again. Kam's face was the picture of defeat recognizing that they didn't know where they were or really where they were going. Reading her, Kai began to nod his head, accepting that they had no choice but to let Bash be their guide, even though he felt a sinking feeling in the pit of his stomach. Mira watched the exchange between the twins and tried to read their body language. From what she could understand from their subtle movements, she knew that they'd all come to an agreement to let Bash be their guide through Pollutio.

"Okay, we will accept you being our guide," Kam said, begrudgingly.

"But don't try any funny business, okay?" Kai warned.

Mira laughed as they settled differences, not understanding the danger she was about to be in.

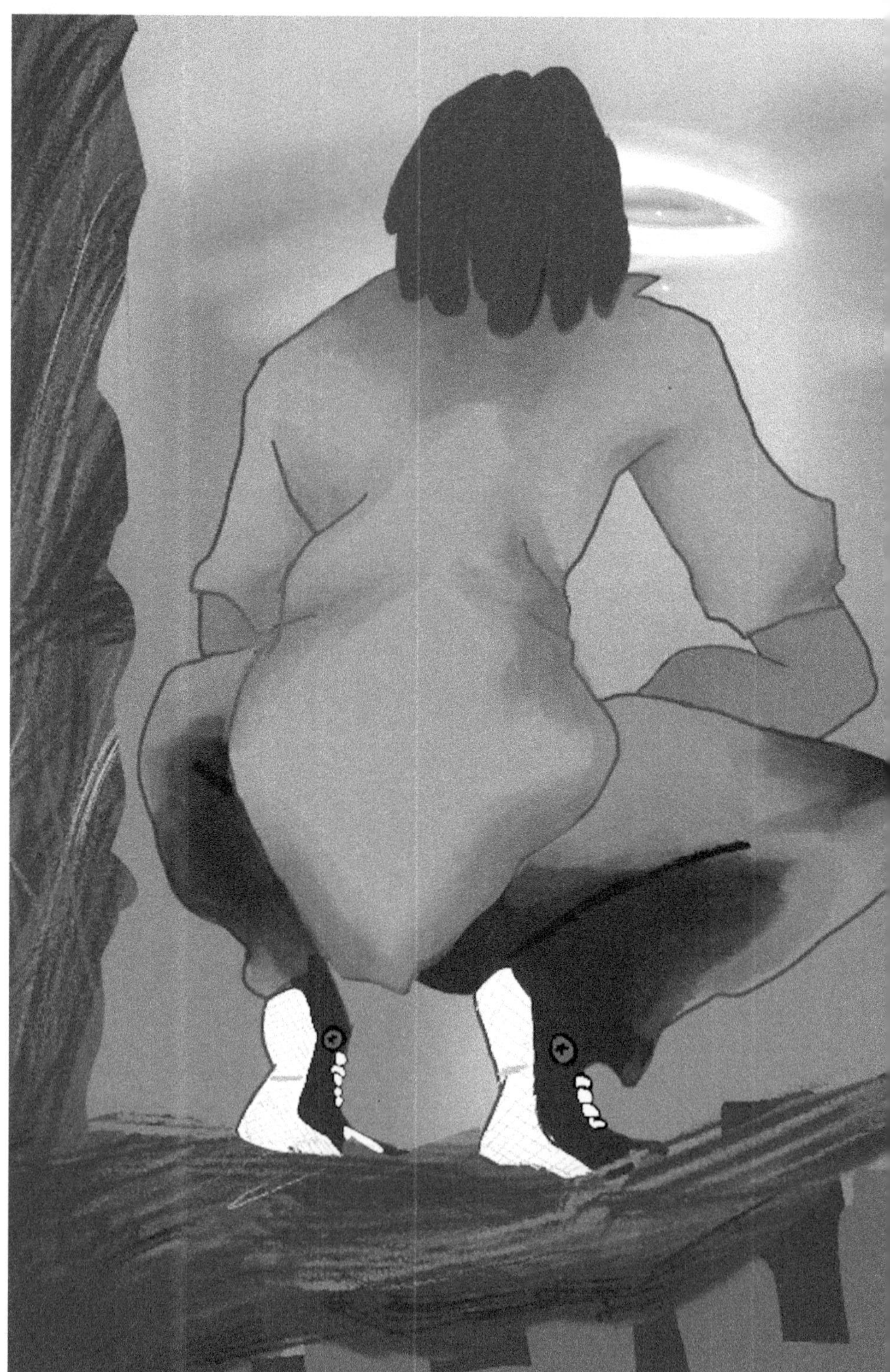

CHAPTER 6

Bash stood in front of a small hut. It was a little broken down with borders around the windows.

"Finally! Home at last!" He shouted, joy flowing through his voice. "Alright, let's head inside," he said.

Bash walked, opening the door to the hut and welcoming the group into his home. Everyone walked in except Mira. Instead, she peered at the interior of the hut in disgust while Kai and Ka followed Bash into the middle of the hut. Mira stayed in the doorway even though Bash began explaining to them more about Pollutio—especially the beast Apollyon.

"The beast has been comin' to this ole place for a while now," Bash said. "He's been terrorizing this place since before I was born."

The twins were stunned by the revelation. "Does this beast have any other worldly powers?" Kam asked Bash, anxiety rising in her voice.

"If ya talking about its magical powers, then yeah," Bash said matter of factly. "One time, that big ole thing burnt down a whole building with just its breath!" he said, turning to face Kam.

So that's why that petrifying feeling has been with us since we got here, Kam thought, using her power of telepathy to communicate with Kai.

Ah, not only that, but our powers have been on the fritz, Kai thought back. But on a more positive note, it seems like when we're far away from the beast, our powers reactivate, even if only a little bit.

Kai and Kam continued their telepathic sidebar.

"So, the Apollyon must also have some magical powers?" Kam assumed. "Is it possible that one of its abilities may be to disrupt any magical energy near its presence or close by to preserve its own?"

Kai said to Kam in his head, That seems to be the case. This ability is in effect when the beast is near anyone else who has magical powers. The further away from it as we can get, the better for us, because the more magic we'll be able to use. Right now, the beast isn't in proximity, so our magic flow is good. But, even with the little bit of power we have, it's not like we'll be able to defeat him.

"Hey, Kam! Hello!" A booming voice invaded Kam's train of thought. She jumped up high into the air, frightened before she realized Bash was speaking to her. Her voice trembled as she said, "Oh, sorry, Bash, can you repeat what you said?"

"Uhh, sure? I guess," Bash said. He repeated the last question of the monologue the twins had missed. "Why do you want the book?"

"Wait, what book?" Kam asked, unable to piece together what Bash had said.

"Ugh, how about you open up those ears of yours!" Bash said, irritation lacing his voice and crisscrossing the smooth planes of his young face.

Mira yelled out loud. In an aggravated tone she said, "The book. Bash is talking about is the book that has some stupid magic writing in it. Apparently the book was located in the town and the Apollyon came looking for it. Blah, blah, blah. He destroyed the town and then took the book with him back to his lair."

Mira summarized what Bash had said about the magical book.

Bash cleared his throat, chuckling nervously. "Yeah, what she said, pretty much. If I remember correctly," he continued, "The Apollyon said something about the book containing some lost or hidden magic. He seemed kinda desperate to get it. I guess he believed that somebody here could use the magic in the book to finally defeat him once and for all, even though no one here knows how to use magic at all. Ha ha." Bash laughed ironically.

"Oh, that book," Kam said, trying to make up for what she hadn't been paying attention to. She pretended to ponder for a moment. "Well, the reason I want the book is because… uh…"

Kam couldn't think of anything to say. She never thought about the book, even with the new information she'd just received. Still, she couldn't come up with a reason she and Kai would need to get the book of lost magic. She figured that even if the book truly contained hidden magical spells, it wasn't like they needed it. They came from a world where magic was always around the corner and always in use.

In Aeolus, there were millions of books, folktales, elders, mages, and witches. That would have all the knowledge they ever needed about magic.

"We want the book because, if we don't help you get it, then the Apollyon will turn this place into his playground and all of you will be his toys, and not in a good way," Kai said, cutting through the silence of Kam's thoughts.

"Oh, that makes sense. Glad to know that you want to help the people of this world," Bash said. He grinned.

"Tch, whatever," Kai said, turning his back to Bash.

"What about you, Mira?" Bash asked, turning to her. "Why do you want the book?"

"Why do I want the book?" Mira asked aloud before pausing for a moment. "Well, you said that the book has magic, and maybe that magic can be used to get me out of this dump and get me back home to Earth." She muttered to herself, "I should have stuck with the group on the field trip at the museum."

Bash didn't hear Mira mumbling to herself. He said reassuringly, "Ah, I'm sure you'll get back to your own world."

"What about you, Bash?" Kam demanded to know. "You've been questioning all of us about our motives for getting this book. What's your reason for desiring the book so badly?"

"Why do I want the book?" Bash repeated. "Ha… that's a long story, but I ran into the Apollyon when I was around the age of seven. I was traveling around, looking at the vast hills of Pollutio's rubble, when I saw some type of black hole pop up. Instead of absorbing things, it spat out the purple beast. He looked a little roughed-up, like he had just gotten into a fight and lost."

Standing in the middle of Bash's modest hut made of compacted, Lego-brick-like trash, Mira, Kai, and Kam listened closely to Bash explain how he watched the Apollyon fall from the sky.

"His eyes were like gems," Bash continued. "They scanned the area before him out of nowhere. Then he launched up and rammed his head into one of the hills of garbage. The hill came crashing down. But that didn't stop her."

Bash paused for a moment in his story as he reflected on the day that his life completely changed. When he went from having just one parent to no parents at all.

Kam zeroed in on the singular detail of Bash's story. Her, she thought to herself. She wanted to know who was this her Bash was referring to. What is her connection to him? Kam continued to ponder about the mysterious woman and what she had to do with the Apollyon. As Kam's thoughts became so engrossed on this one detail Bash shared, she missed many others.

"Ever since then, the Apollyon has taken the book for himself," Bash said, wrapping up his story. "Nothing's happened yet, so I guess he doesn't know how to use it, but we still need to get that book away from him and get you guys back to your worlds."

Mira and Kai nodded their heads in agreement with Bash while Kam looked confused and dumbfounded where she stood, trying to piece together what she missed.

"Alright, so it's settled," Kai said. "The beast has some magical powers we need to work around. Me and Kam will fight him, but with most of our powers on the fritz, it's not a guaranteed defeat."

With the twins unable to access the full range of their telepathy or summon the divinations from their weapons and still untrained on how to control their incantations, they knew they needed to innovate and figure out how to defeat the Apollyon.

Bash said, "I have a few weapons that I made myself. They're not professional, but they'll do something."

"Although this may be futile, Kam and I can hold the beast off. During that time, Bash, you and Mira need to skate by and find the book. Once you two have secured the book, you'll need to escape quickly. We'll try our best to hold the Apollyon back," Kai said.

"So that's the plan," Kam said. "We'll head in, and me and Kai will engage the Apollyon. Bash and Mira can stay back and grab the book."

Everyone seemed pleased with this plan.

"Is everyone ready?" Kam asked, taking charge of the group.

Everyone nodded as they left the hut, prepared to fight the wild Apollyon.

CHAPTER 7

Kai, Kam, Mira, and Bash set out on their journey to look for the book of lost magic in the post-apocalyptic society. The journey on Pollutio was made ten times harder because of the massive amount of compact trash they had to wade through. Surprisingly, Bash lived in a cleaner area of the realm among the trash from Earth that was still as dirty and teeming high as a landfill.

The four maneuvered carefully through the area, looking high and low and around every little hut their eyes could see across the vast land. They were trying to gather clues that would lead them to the book. Eventually, they traveled down a road-like structure made between the mounds of trash by the people of Pollutio. Mira and Bash led the search while the twins followed close behind. Along their journey, Kai, Kam, and Mira spotted a shiny object peeking out beneath one of the mounds of trash. They were intrigued and believed it could be a clue for where the book could be. Believing that maybe the stories of the Apollyon possessing the book could have been false. But Bash wasn't so convinced. He knew from living all of his life on Pollutio that the shiny object they spotted could very well be a trap.

"We don't have time to investigate what that is," Bash said as he tried to keep their search party going where he was leading them.

"Why?" Mira asked, intrigued by the shimmer of the still-unknown object.

"Because it could be a trap. It could cause trouble," Bash said.

Kai and Kam understood Bash's hesitance. They listened to his words and continued to follow him as he walked off, desperate to move away from the object. But Mira, stubborn as she was, didn't agree with Bash. Just like she'd left her classmates in the gardens of the Cummer Museum, Mira dug in her heels and refused to listen to reason. Being her typical self, she decided to move closer and look at the object alone, satisfied in her ignorance to the events that would follow her brazen action.

Closer and closer, Mira inched toward the object until she noticed someone was touching her.

"Mira!" Bash screamed as he hurriedly ran towards her. But Mira was too engrossed in her own mission. Too focused, obsessed with wanting and needing to know what the object was, that she didn't hear Bash yelling her name.

"Why did you pull me away?" Mira shouted at Bash once he reached her. "I almost touched it."

"You can't touch that," Bash said with a frustrated anger present in his voice. "It's too dangerous. You don't know what kind of creature may appear when you touch that thing."

Mira was angry too. She seethed in her feelings like one of the cartoon characters she'd watched as a child on Earth that blew smoke through its ears when mad. She hung back behind Kai, Kam, and Bash, furious over being pulled away from what she wanted to do. I don't care what he says, Mira thought to herself once the three were far enough ahead of her.

Ignoring Bash's warning, Mira turned around and went and pulled the object out to get a better look at it. It looked to Mira like a crushed soda can. She was so engrossed in her investigation of the item that reminded her of home that she didn't notice Kai and Kam turning to each other with horror rippling across their young faces. They saw first what Bash and Mira had yet to see for themselves.

"Mo-mo-mo-mo-monster," the twins stuttered in fear.

Bash turned around as fast as a helicopter propeller and looked at the creature, eye to eye.

"Guys, I want you to run in the other direction and not look back," he said as calmly as possible.

The twins ran off first. Mira sensed the atmosphere had changed around her. She looked up from the object she was holding to see Bash standing between her and the monster. She dropped the object and followed behind Kai and Kam, finally listening to Bash.

With his new friends safe, Bash turned back to the monster, ready to defeat it. But he hesitated. Instead, he had another idea that would involve losing something he had been waiting for for so long. Eye to eye with another treacherous creature, Bash decided right then and there that he was done dealing with the Apollyon.

Satisfied with his decision to not engage in a fight with the Apollyon, Bash rushed to catch up to find Kai, Kam, and Mira. When he reached them, they were back inside his hut. Mira heard the sounds of Bash's heavy boots walking up first. She ran outside, provoked by her anger, still unhappy but this time for a different reason.

"Why didn't you tell me to not touch the object?" she yelled in her outburst. "You could have gotten all of us killed."

Bash clenched his jaw and balled his fists at his side. He was aggravated with Mira's selfishness and angry that not only had she not listened to him, but that she had the nerve to blame others when she decided to act on her own instead of going through with his original plan.

"Mira, you know what? I'm fed up with you!" Bash yelled back at her. "All I have done is try to help you and the twins, and this is how you talk to me? You were the one who could have killed us. You are a very selfish person. You can't even get along with yourself, so I'm done helping YOU!"

Mira, embarrassed to be the target of Bash's anger, stormed off into the realm of trash without saying a single word to the other three. Kai and Kam just looked at each other, unsure of what to do next. Bash stayed put where he was just outside his hut. He was surprised by his own anger and the words that left his mouth.

"Maybe we should go after her," the twins said in unison, after a few uncomfortable moments had passed.

Bash shook his head "no." He refused.

"Let Mira be. Let her cool down and be alone for a while," Bash said.

Kai and Kam had no choice but to agree. They didn't know that Bash had let the monster go free. It was still roaming around, and Bash knew it was only a matter of time before Mira would be taken by the monster. That will keep him busy, Bash thought to himself.

He knew it was important to keep the Apollyon busy because with him occupied with Mira for the rest of the night, Bash would be able to get into the monster's lair to grab the book.

"Guys, I have bad news," Bash said, deciding to let the twins in on his plan. "Mira is going to be taken by the monster from earlier because I didn't defeat him."

Bash hesitated as he watched Kai and Kam's faces go wide with surprise. They looked at him curiously, waiting for him to drop the true reason they'd been feeling unsettled since they arrived.

"I let him go," Bash said finally.

Kai and Kam looked from Bash to each other and back again without speaking. Shock slowly registered across their faces as they realized what he'd done.

We never should have trusted him, Kai and Kam said to each other through their telepathy.

Kai tightened his grip on his sword as Kam reached behind her back for a bow and arrow.

"Stop," Kai said, communicating only with his sister. "He's our only hope."

Kam dropped her arms back to her side, realizing her brother was right. Her face slack and arms loose, she tried not to show the defeat she felt. Instead, she turned from Kai to Bash, feeling resolved about what they needed to do.

"Well, let's go save her," Kam said, ignoring the feeling in the pit of her stomach. "Come on!"

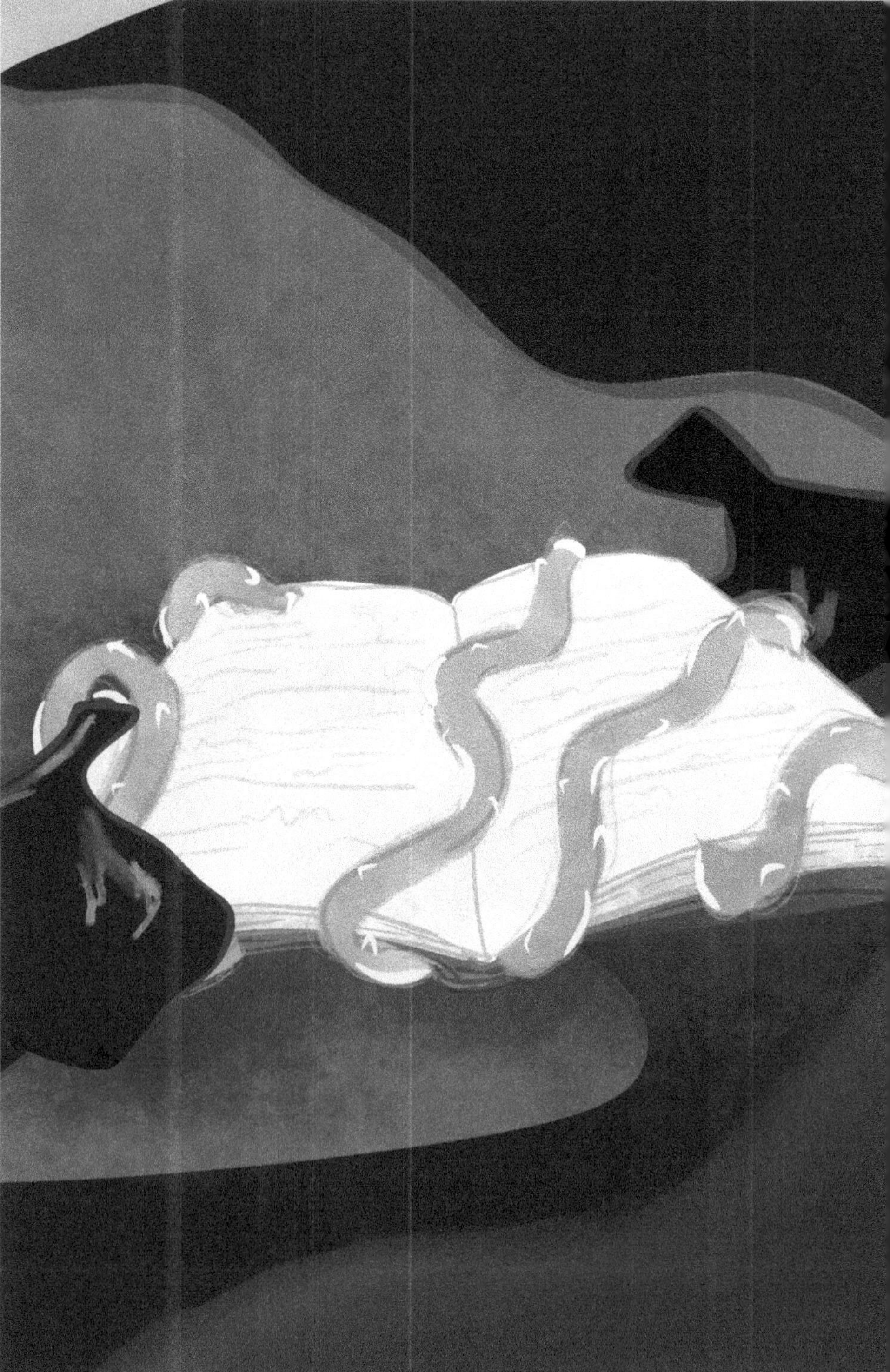

CHAPTER 8

Bash led the way for Kai and Kam. "This way," he said. "We are almost there."

It was late at night as the three walked to the monster's lair to save their lost companion, Mira.

"Do you guys have your weapons ready?" Bash asked. "When we go in the cave, we have to be prepared for whatever may be in there."

Kai held up his sword and Kam gripped her bow and arrows in hand, ready for the attack. Bash had his heavy metal staff ready too. The three of them crept into the cave. The monster was sleeping on the ground next to what looked like its working area, the place where it stored its collected items.

"Hey you, wake up!" Bash yelled. "Where is our friend?"

Kam held her bow ready to aim with an arrow pulled taut, ready to attack. The Apollyon got up like an angry baby being awakened from a nap.

"What is the meaning of this encounter?" the Apollyon demanded to know. "What friend do you speak of? Is it that stubborn girl I captured tonight? Is she the one you speak of?"

The Apollyon, a dark purple beast, was fifteen feet tall, wings on protruding from his back. He cackled to himself. He had two pairs of arms with sharp claws like blades and long creepy eyes that looked like a carnelian. His eyes glowed so bright that they stood out like a sore thumb.

"Where is she?" Kai demanded with his sword drawn, ready to attack. "Where is she? We don't have time for your games. Why did you take her in the first place?"

Kai yelled his barrage of questions at the monster, who just laughed in their faces as he rolled around on the ground of his lair.

"She is being prepared for my dinner tomorrow," the monster managed through its fitful laughter.

"Dinner?" the twins exclaimed in unison.

Bash didn't say a word to the monster. Kai and Kam looked at him as his mind seemed to wander away from the high-stakes encounter with the monster. Instead, Bash looked around the cave for a while until he spotted something of interest. It was the book of lost magic he had mentioned to the twins and Mira.

"Guys, draw your weapons. This conversation is getting us nowhere," Kam said, annoyed with the apparent stalemate. She looked around to see if her brother and Bash were prepared to fight. That was when she noticed Bash standing near the monster's junk.

"Bash, what are you doing?" she yelled. "We have to save Mira first. Her life is more important than the book."

Kai and Kam both looked at Bash with confusion as he ignored them and moved closer toward stealing the book from the monster. The twins watched with their weapons drawn as they tried to keep their attention on the Apollyon to keep him from getting away.

"Guys, the book is more important and will help you get back home," Bash said. He tried to plead his case and explain his actions. "It's right here. Come on." he urged.

"No! We can't leave her." Kai said.

Bash ignored Kai. While the twins had the Apollyon cornered with their weapons, Bash walked over to the collected items in the lair, grabbed the book for himself, and then walked out of the cave.

"We thought we could trust you," the twins cried out after Bash.

They watched as Bash left them, angered and hurt by the betrayal. But they couldn't focus on their own feelings. They twins didn't forget about their mission. They didn't give up on Mira. They understood that they were on their own and they would have to fight the Apollyon anyway.

"Ha ha ha ha." The Apollyon laughed in their faces. "You guys think you can beat me? Think again."

"There is only one way we'll find out," Kai said, ready for war.

CHAPTER 9

The twins stood in their fighting stance, five feet away from the Apollyon. It felt like seconds had turned into minutes, and minutes into hours. It was deathly silent in the monster's lair. They all eyed each other, anticipating who would make the first move. Even the air felt hotter to Kai and Kam, and their bodies began to perspire in places not easily seen. They felt their sweat form, bead, and trickle about their body, insulating them with their own nervous anxiety. Was this because of the dreaded threat looming over them? Were they anxious about the outcome of their battle ahead?

Instantly, the Apollyon cut through the silence and the distance between him and the twins, undeterred by the weapons aimed at his face. With a slash of his arm, the Apollyon struck Kai. Kai's body was flung ten feet backwards through the air from the feedback from the Apollyon's arm. The feedback was so strong that it should have killed him. When he finally hit the ground, he was like a piece of trash being discarded. With his sword shattered into pieces all over the ground, Kai struggled to get up from the attack. His mind raced and his vision seemed to be cut, as if he had gone completely blind. All he could see was white. A strong gust of wind came over him. Kai struggled to catch his breath. It felt as if he was losing oxygen and nothing in his body was working as it should.

"Ah! Ah! Ah!" Kai grunted in agony.

SLAP!

"Pull yourself together!" Kam yelled, her voice full of distress. She had fled away from the Apollyon, ignoring the fact that her backside was exposed. Her focus was solely on her injured brother.

Kai blinked. His vision returned to him, he could see his sister. He launched to his feet, forgetting his pain.

"Kam, we need to do something, and do it quickly!" Kai wailed at Kam.

"You need to stay back and catch your breath. I'll fight the Apollyon myself," she said assuredly.

Observing her twin, Kam noticed that Kai's eyes looked as if they were asking "why," but Kam felt she had no reason to explain herself. Her heart raced. For the first time, she felt weaker than the opponent she was facing. Not only that, she felt the agony her brother was going through. She didn't like the fact that he looked so weak. Kam was afraid that this may be the end for her brother, but there was no more time for her to think about her own feelings.

Kam turned her back on her brother and ran off toward the purple beast. The fifteen-foot distance was nothing for her. With just a few steps, Kam propelled herself forward. Everything in her body was pushing itself to the absolute limit. Her body was like a jet stream as it closed the distance between the purple beast and herself.

Drawing back, the beast prepared to strike Kam with its claw. The claw came down like an axe, but Kam managed to dodge the attack. She prepared an arrow and tried to aim for the Apollyon's gem-like eyes. But the Apollyon possessed the power of intuition. He sensed her attack and used another one of his arms to strike Kam from her side. Her body flew 40 feet into the air. This height should have killed her, but she just barely survived. In mid-air, Kam tried to catch herself, but she was hit by another attack by the Apollyon. She slammed to the ground. The impact caused her body to bounce back up, and she momentarily lost consciousness.

As she started to regain her senses, she noticed that her ears were ringing. It was like a bell had been installed inside her eardrum. Kam tried her best to shake away the sound and maneuver despite the pain she felt. Once she was finally able to stand, Kam limped a little. Her hands were in the position as if she was preparing to shoot an arrow from her bow, but they were empty.

The Apollyon walked towards her, smirking. "Hmm, where's that spunk you just had? Ha ha ha ha!"

The Apollyon looked down on her. Standing at his full fifteen feet of height, he smirked, believing she was nothing more than a fly buzzing around his ear.

Kam had a headache. Her thoughts were focused on nothing but survival. She couldn't give up.

"This may be the attack that ends it all," she heard Kai say behind her.

Kam jerked her head back to see Kai walking toward her and the Apollyon.

"Kam, there's one attack I know will seal the deal," Kai said.

He clenched his fists. Kai's eyes gleamed with determination. His surefire plan was a secret technique passed down from the twins' family. A magical incantation that would override any cursed magic. But there was a cost for using it. They would experience a severe amount of pain because they had not yet learned how to control their ancestral power. It was like a ticking time bomb. Once the fuse was lit, the user willing to speak the incantation had no choice but to commit to the plan. Kai was committed, even though he knew that there had been members of his own royal family who had been completely broken by this technique.

"Are you serious?" Kam exclaimed when she realized what Kai was going to do. "That move is dangerous, and we haven't even learned how to control it."

She completely shut down the idea of using the technique.

Kai was adamant. "I know you're right. This move is dangerous, but I'm not asking you to do it because I know it could completely destroy me. I'm praying for a miracle that may not be heard. I know it's a dream that I can't make come true, but I won't give up," Kai shouted back.

His voice and tone told Kam that he was dead-set on his plan.

"I'm going to defeat the beast, Kam. If you want to stay back, then that's fine. I'll be okay as long as you make it out of here."

Kai had accepted his fate. He knew that if he didn't want the Apollyon to destroy everything, he would have to recite the incantation. Even if it meant his body would be destroyed and he would completely lose his mind.

"I'll bear it somehow," Kai whispered to himself.

He walked away from Kam, marching toward the Apollyon. Kam looked down. She trembled from the top of her head to the soles of her feet.

"Fi... fine," she stuttered. "I won't let you bear that pain alone."

A tear fell from her eye and rolled across her cheek. She ran toward her brother. Catching up to him, she said, "Let's do this together! This was entrusted to us."

Kai looked at his sister. His eyes widened with joy and a smile came across his face. "Right!" he exclaimed.

Kai suggested that they recite the incantation together. Their breathing synced, their heartbeats pounded in time together. Even their sweat seemed to drip down their bodies in anxious harmony as their thoughts aligned. The twins inhaled and exhaled and began reciting the incantation.

Flawless and Firm
Climbing the hill toward twilight's burn

Surviving countless battlefields
Wielding minds and might of steel

Marching onward
Carrying generations
Doubt cast away
We strike with no hesitation

Gaze upon our resolve
Soar into the sky, reaching for Aeolus heavens above

Come forth, our realization
Bind our power in this incantation

In an instant, Kai and Kam's perspective changed to pure white. A strong gust of wind pushed the twins backward, and they struggled to stand up. They couldn't move. Even lifting a finger was a struggle for them. Kam clenched her teeth and tried to push her body forward. Kai clenched his fists and tried to run through the wind. Their efforts were useless. Their vision faded away and the rush of wind ruptured their eardrums. But then they saw it. Through the gust of wind was a golden light. They barely had a glimpse, but the sighting gave them the strength they needed to push through. Their vision fired up, and both of their bodies were cut through by the wind like a giant axe. When Kai and Kam reached the golden light, silence surrounded them. They stood together, their grayish-hair glowing with then golden light shrouding them like halos. Kai and Kam lifted their arms, forcing all of the power of their magic into their arms.

"Ah," they grunted in agony.

The precautions the twins had overlooked came back. Their bodies ached in pain, but they had to push forward. The magical energy flowing from them punished their physical bodies with its recoil. But the twins didn't care. They had no worry. They focused their undivided attention on the Apollyon, who hadn't moved yet but seemed prepared for anything. The Apollyon stared at the twins, full of hostility. It recognized their use of magic.

Moving its eyes, the Apollyon said, "Ho… how… can you two use magic? My presence should dull your senses, quench your powers, and make you incapable of such feats."

The twins did not respond. Then, a huge gust of wind burst from the area. This power wasn't from the Apollyon. It was from the twins. A shape began to form in the twins' hands. The Apollyon was shoved down by the huge gust of wind.

One second.

A ball of golden light formed before them.

Two seconds.

The ball of light formed into the family's crest of a large star and two intertwining lines that met in the middle. Kai and Kam's bodies and mind were constantly breaking, and the surge of energy from the incantation was becoming harder to bear, along with the physical agony the twins were in.

Three seconds.

The Apollyon, who was thrown off balance by the surge of the twins combining power, charged up and dashed up off of the ground. He lifted his massive arm up in the air and prepared to strike the twins down.

Four seconds.

The Apollyon closed the gap, and the twins stepped forward, confronting him. They stood before him, gazing up as he grimaced from his full fifteen feet of height. The muscles of his upper and lower arms flexed. The twins even noticed breath circulating through his body as his windpipe vibrated as he regulated his breathing. At his temple, they noticed a steady tick like a vein pulsing with rage. At their own eye level, all they could see were his legs taut in the stance, ready to attack. The twins took aim at twelve targets and launched the golden star that formed from the glowing golden ball of light in their hands toward the beast.

"Ahhhhhhhhh!" the twins screamed together in unison.

The star jolted forward toward the beast at an incredible speed, striking the Apollyon and hitting all twelve of its targets at once.

"Roarrrrrrrrrrrrr!"

The Apollyon grunted away in agony as the light from the star surrounded its lair. In the light, Kai and Kam could clearly see their surroundings. The image was shocking. The Apollyon remained standing, although his body was severely damaged. His upper arms had been severed off. His lower arms were dangling by the tendons. The magical crest they had launched was strong, but not strong enough. Kai and Kam were dumbfounded. There was nothing else they could do. The magical energy that overflowed through their body had dispersed out of them.

"Ha ha ha!" The Apollyon laughed at the twins. "That one actually stung a little. Good one. Just for that, I think you two deserve a reward."

The Apollyon lifted his torn arm and grabbed the twins. Their bodies were burnt from reciting the incantation, which took hold of them once again and left them both wracked with pain. Kam collapsed in The Apollyon's large claw when he grabbed her. Kai fought to keep his consciousness, but he failed. The twins were defeated by the Apollyon. They too were now its prisoners along with Mira.

CHAPTER 10

Bash sprinted back home, ignoring the howls from Kai and Kam about leaving them to fight the Apollyon. He held the book tightly in his hands until his knuckles turned white.

"Yes! The book of lost magic is mine, finally, after all these years!" Bash said excitedly.

Bash made it back to his hut and quickly sat on his couch, which was nothing more than a few cubes of trash he had put together to sit on. The couch was so wrecked that it was almost coming apart, holding at the seams of the thread he had used to stitch it together.

"I can't believe I got it! After all these years, it's finally in my hands!" Bash shouted at the top of his lungs. "After all these years, Mama, your dream will finally come true."

Thinking of his mom, Bash paused. He gazed at the dusty book in his hand, his mind overflowing with distant memories of his mother. He remembered spending time with her, her smile shining like the rising sun, and her constant generosity always helping the deprived and sickly.

His mother had done her best to make sure everyone experienced an ideal life in such a cruel and unforgiving world. Although she never possessed any riches, her benevolent heart had changed the lives of many with her offerings of food and shelter. Bash thought of his mother until his precious memories nearly overwhelmed his mind. But as he thought about her, one memory stuck out to him like a sore thumb.

Tears poured down from his mother's face, and Bash remembered the tightness that had overtaken his throat and his chest. It was like he was suffocating. His mother was crying over the death of his father; her lover. The rugged world of Pollutio had bared its sharp fangs, and Bash's father died after a long battle with an unknown illness that wracked his body with so much fever and consumption that he rotted from the inside out. Bash and his mother watched his father's decay every day before their eyes. When he finally died, they were both engulfed by their agony.

Bash had watched his mother mourn. He felt helpless. He wanted to do something for the woman who had put everyone else's needs before her own, including his father's. He ran to his mother and hugged her. He tried to offer her comfort the best way he knew how.

"It's okay, mama. You still have me!" Bash recalled saying to her in the wake of his father's death.

But he couldn't keep himself composed. Tears had oozed from his eyes. Instead of Bash comforting his mother, it was his mother who ended up comforting him once again. She set aside all the sorrow she felt for her own loss and gave all of her attention to her son. Bash wondered why she so suddenly seemed to stop mourning her loss. Was it because it was her duty as a mother? Or was it because that was just the kind of person she was? A woman who would give up the world to save one person?

It was only recently that Bash began to ask himself these questions. In thinking about his mother, Bash felt her warmth wrap around him. In that moment, he made it his goal to become just like his mother, to protect those around him and to put a smile on everyone's face. That was who Bash thought he'd become when he was just six years old.

Why? Why? Did I give up on that goal? Bash questioned himself. He tried to find the moment when he had changed. Looking back on his childhood, he realized how idealistic he had been about the world up until his parents died, one after the other. As a child, though he lived in a dump of a world where people needed to rob each other to survive, he believed then that those wouldn't always be his circumstances. With his father dying of sickness and his mother being killed shortly after, he remembered that that was when he began to change.

Now at sixteen years old, he knew the answer to end his struggles and return to his childhood ideals. When his mother had first heard the rumors about a "wish-granting book," she set off to find it for herself. She and Bash explored day in and day out, trying to find the magical book. It didn't take long for Bash to remember why his mother had wanted the book.

"Because if this book can truly grant wishes, Bash, then maybe mama can make this world perfect for everyone," he recalled her saying. "Think about it!

No more stealing others' food. No more looking for spare scraps. No more fighting to live another day. We can all live together in peace!"

Bash remembered the excitement his mother's voice had held. It burst through her and radiated throughout her entire body. That was why she didn't back down from the Apollyon when she had encountered it. The book had been right there in a field near the Apollyons's lair. Her goal, her dream, her desire was right there, and she was so close to it. Only the Apollyon stood in her way. And although the mighty beast stood in front of her, she was not willing to back down.

In the field filled with hills of scraps, the Apollyon and Bash's mother fought. The Apollyon knocked over a hill. Bash's mother shoved him away from the falling mountain of trash, sacrificing herself to save him.

Bash shook his head to clear the memories of his mother's final moments, her last act in service to another. To him.

Sitting on the couch in his hut, Bash stared at the book of lost magic. Tears gushed from his eyes. He was choked up, thinking about his mother's sacrifice and how he had so easily given up on his friends for his selfish goal. Bash knew that his mother never would have sacrificed anyone else for her own greed.

"Mama, your dream was to make a perfect world," Bash said aloud. "Well, a world without my friends is a terrible world."

Bash stood up from the couch, walked to the side of his hut, and grabbed two staffs made of disposed scraps. He put them in the back of his shirt and threw the book down.

"I'm coming, y'all!" Bash yelled.

He dashed out of his hut. His mind was set on saving his friends no matter what. He ran all the way to the Apollyon's lair, ready for the final battle.

"I'm such an idiot. Why did I do that?" He questioned himself on his journey. "I shouldn't have left the twins and Mira in the cave with that monster. Even if they are warriors, they are not used to the evils of this world, but I am!"

Nearing the Apollyon's cave, Bash shouted aloud to himself, "Hope you guys can forgive me after this!" He hoped his words would make it all the way to Kai, Kam and Mira.

CHAPTER 11

Mira kicked the prison cell wall and let out a frustrated growl before plopping down into a corner, pouting.

"Ugh!" she moaned. "This is all their fault! If they had only listened to me, none of this would've happened!" She punched the wall beside her with the side of her fist. "Maybe if the twins weren't so reckless... maybe if Bash wasn't such a— wait. Bash. It's his fault! He sold us out to the monster! That little —"

Mira could feel a sense of anger, frustration, and betrayal flowing through her. She felt her face get hot with rage. She kicked around the dirt and rubble and threw a temper tantrum like she always did when she was home and didn't get her way on Earth. She continued with her irrational outburst for nearly ten minutes, but to her it felt like thirty seconds. When she finally settled down, she plopped back down into her little corner, realizing there was nothing she could do. She was trapped in a cell. A prisoner in the Apollyon's lair. Mira closed her eyes and sighed.

Why did this have to happen to me? Mira thought to herself. She began to think about how she might be able to get out of the prison cell. Instead, she was besieged by thoughts and memories of her own bad behavior.

Was I a little ungrateful? Yes. Was I bratty? Yes. Was I rude? Yes. But do I deserve to be locked up in a dark cell, threatened by a monster who could enter and eat me at any given time? No.

Mira buried her head into her knees and clenched her fists. A rush of sadness came upon her. Mira began to cry. If she ever found a way to leave that lair, she promised, deep in her heart, that she would never take anything for granted ever again.

"I haven't been the best person lately," Mira said aloud, admitting to her faults. "No wonder Bash sold us out to the monster. I was so mean to him." Mira went on whispering solemnly to herself. "But I'm going to do better... once I get out of here."

Emboldened by her remorse, Mira stood up from her little corner and walked over to the tall bars that enclosed the cell determined to find a way out. She reached her hand through and tried to squeeze her body out between the bars. She failed. Mira went back to her corner to plot another way to escape, but so many depressing thoughts filled her head.

Why hasn't anyone come to get me? Mira asked herself. My friends from school probably aren't worried about me, and neither is Bash. Maybe because I always push people away.

Mira couldn't think straight. Discouraged, she knew that at the rate she was going, it would be a long while before she finally came up with another plan. A plan she didn't know would inevitably fail because the cell she was being held in was especially designed to keep even the smartest and strongest person from escaping.

CHAPTER 12

Standing outside the Apollyon's lair, Bash convinced himself of what he was about to do.

"Alright," he said, under his breath. "The twins had no choice but to fight the monster alone. They're probably captured by now, along with Mira. I have the book, so that's good. Now I need to come up with a plan to save the three of them."

Bash walked around for a good thirty minutes. In the field where his mother had sacrificed herself for him, Bash remembered how she used to go out of her way to help people survive on Pollutio. How can I help Mira, Kai, and Kam? Bash asked himself as he racked his brain, trying to come up with a plan to save his friends.

"That's it!" he exclaimed. "I'll wait until the monster is asleep, and then I'll pass by it and save them," Bash said.

Still being cautious, Bash collected his staff, nails, and a sheet of rusted metal to use as a shield to help protect himself in case the Apollyon was a light sleeper. When he finished collecting the items he needed, Bash headed for the monster's lair. He arrived at the mouth of the cave and crept a few inches inside as quietly as he could.

"Okay, the Apollyon is sleeping," Bash whispered to himself.

As he looked around his surroundings, Bash noticed a path and a ring of keys. Bash put his thieving skills to use and snagged the keys stored in the Apollyon's collection piles where he had taken the book of lost magic earlier. With the keys safely in his possession, Bash decided to follow the path. He spied to see where it led. As he walked, he saw rows of cells that seemed to go on forever.

"Dang, this cave is huge," Bash said quietly in surprise.

Wandering down the path, Bash finally saw Mira and the twins.

"Bash, you came to save us!" Mira screamed.

Mira was happy to see Bash, but the twins were not. "His conscience was probably eating him up," Kai muttered. "That's the only reason he came back."

Mira looked around, confused.

"Oh, yeah, we didn't tell you how we also got captured," Kam chimed in. "Our lovely friend Bash decided to leave us to the Apollyon so he could steal the book for himself."

Mira looked at Bash in disbelief. Upset by what she'd just heard about him, it didn't outweigh the fact that she was still happy to see him.

"Guys, I'm sorry," Bash began. "But I wanted to make sure you guys were okay, so I came back. Let's go before the Apollyon wakes up."

Bash took his staff and nails he had armed himself with just outside the Apollyon's lair. He noticed that around him on the ground were Kai's shattered sword and Kam's bow and quiver full of arrows. He smiled, picked up Kam's bow and arrows, and handed them to her.

"Kai and Kam, I got your weapons back," Bash said with a smile.

Using the keys he swiped from the Apollyon's collections, Bash released Mira, Kai, and Kam. Finally free, instead of thanking him, Kai and Kam snatched their weapons and walked past Bash, intentionally bumping his shoulders to make him fall.

"Thanks, Bash," Mira said in a quiet, timid voice. Even though she was hurt that Bash had left them to die, she believed he couldn't have done it for no reason.

"I'm so sorry, again." Bash apologized as Mira, Kai, and Kam walked away from him. "I really don't know what came over me."

"I do," Kam said, whirling around. "Greed and selfishness."

Bash stayed silent because he couldn't argue with the facts. As the four of them walked back to the entrance of the cave, it seemed to Bash like it was darker than when he first entered.

"Guys, something is off. Be ready for anything," Bash warned as the foreboding feeling settled deep within him.

"Last time you said that, you ran off," Kai mocked.

They kept walking until they reached the place where the monster was supposedly sleeping.

"Ha ha ha," he laughed, leaping to his feet. "So you came to take away my breakfast, lunch, and dinner?" the monster asked Bash through an angry smile.

The group, confused by the monster's mismatched reaction, drew their weapons, ready to attack.

"Okay, Mira, stay behind me," Bash ordered. "Kai and Kam, I want you guys to help me surround Mira and protect her, but also protect yourselves. The monsters of Pollutio all have the same weak spot between their eyes."

"Perfect. Thanks for the information," Kai said, running toward the monster at full speed and swinging his sword.

Kai missed landing the first strike of his sword, but he tried again, never letting down his guard.

"I can't reach the eye! It's too tall," Kai yelled to Kam and Bash.

"Kam, protect Mira," Bash said.

He went for the attack with his rusted staff and punted its sharpened javelin tip toward the Apollyon's eye. But it was just too far. The spear hit the side of the cave.

"It's my turn now," Kam said. Standing guard in front of Mira, she pulled an arrow out of the quiver she had slung across her back and focused her aim on one of the Apollyon's long bejeweled eyes.

She coached herself. "Steady, steady, and... bullseye!"

Kam successfully hit the monster in the eye. The Apollyon doubled over in pain and yelped, "You dumb kids! How dare you hurt me."

The Apollyon screamed in agony, but still with that weird smile that seemed almost painted on its face.

"Let's go! Hurry up, while it's distracted," Mira yelled in amazement at all the brave fighting that had taken place. What she had seen was something she'd normally only watched in movies, but now she had witnessed it in real life. Together, Mira, Bash, Kai, and Kam ran out of the cave as fast as they could and headed back to Bash's hut.

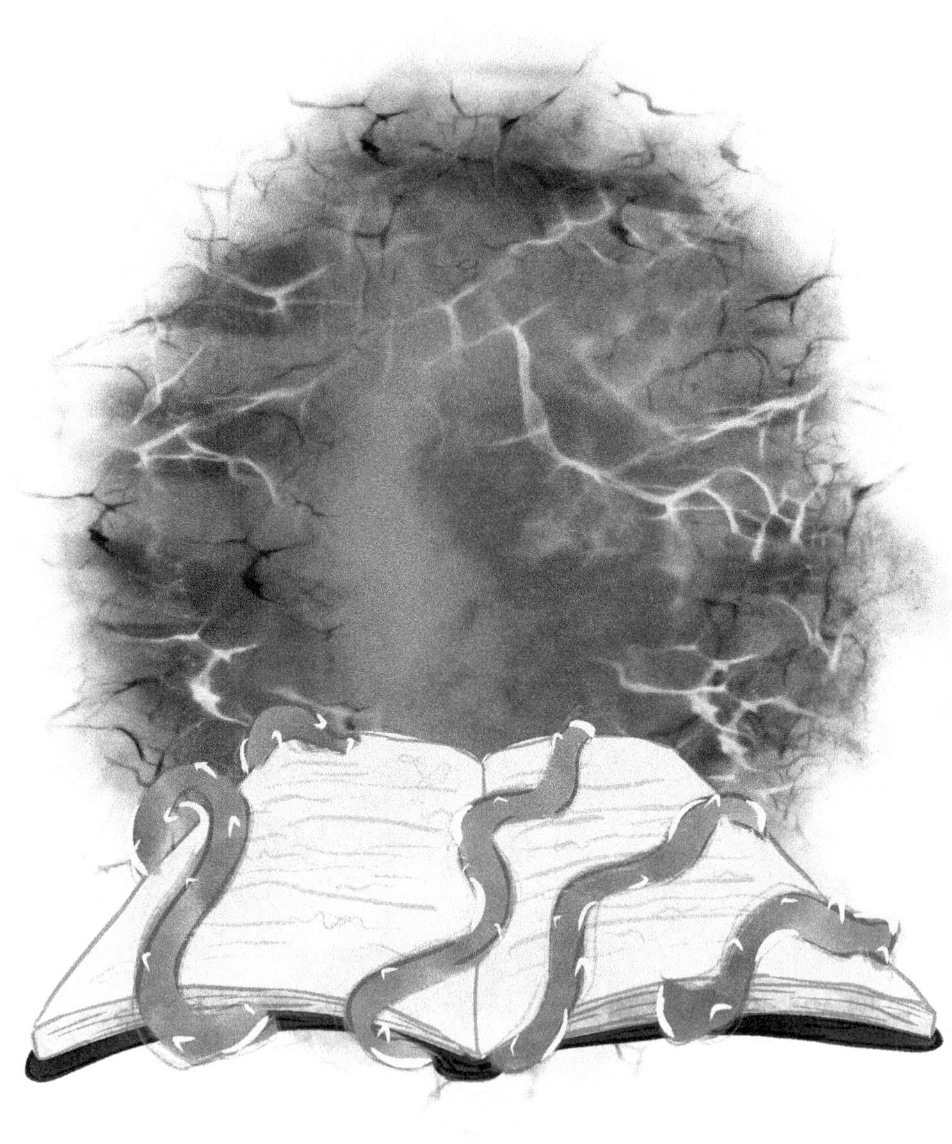

CHAPTER 13

Everyone cheered.

"Whooo! We did it," Kai screamed excitedly.

But despite the jubilant voices the atmosphere was still filled with the tension from Bash's betrayal.

"I just want to say that I'm still very sorry for what I did," Bash said, sensing the mood. "I know it —"

"Bash, we aren't mad at you. Just a little hurt," Kam said, cutting him off. "But of course we are happy that you decided to come back for us."

Kam flashed her brightest smile to let Bash know that she meant what she said. Kai moved in for a hug, sensing that Bash was hurting and that was what had made him take the book of lost magic. Mira followed the twins and wrapped her arms around Bash, too. It was a group hug among the four of them, all of them happy that they had made it out alive and away from the monster's lair.

"Now let's open up this book and see how to get you guys home," Bash said, pumped.

"How, umm, do we use this thing?" Mira asked, confused.

Bash looked at Mira and then at the book. "Well, you see, I know about the book, but not really how to use it, but let's see," he said bashfully.

Bash flipped through the book, looking for any clue on how to activate its magic. Going through page after page, Bash finally found a puzzle that had to be drawn out to reveal a portal. But it was incomplete.

"We were so close," Kai wailed. "How are we supposed to find the other piece of the puzzle now? We are never going back home."

"Is nothing else in there?" Kam asked. "Make sure."

"I'm sure," Bash said, flipping through the book once again to make sure he didn't miss anything.

Kai turned around in despair and banged his head against the wall of the hut.

"Wait!" Bash exclaimed. "Kai, what is that on the back of your head? Kam, do you have the same birthmark too?"

"Yes. Why?" Kam asked curiously.

"Hold on—can you turn around for me, next to your brother?" Bash asked.

Bash held up the book and saw that the book's puzzle connected to the birthmark on the backs of the twins' heads. "You guys complete the book. It's a match!"

Bash jumped up and down with excitement. The twins turned back around to face him. Confusion was written all over their faces.

Kam spoke first. "But we have never been here before. How can that be?"

"Well, this book is the book of lost magic," Bash emphasized. "It comes from… I believe, a Kingdom called… Aeolus," Bash stammered.

"That is the name of our kingdom," Kai said.

"Well, let's draw this puzzle out," Mira finally spoke up. "Does it matter where we do it?"

Bash looked through the book again to see if there were any special instructions about how to draw out the puzzle to open the portal. "No, it just says to draw out the puzzle and the book is at your pleasure," Bash answered. "It also says make sure you name where you would like to go above the portal."

Mira grabbed a stick and drew out the puzzle as close as to the images in the book as she could, looking from the book to the twins' heads and back again.

"Okay, I'm done. Now—"

Before Mira could finish her sentence, a blue circle appeared before them with a small key inside of it.

"All we have to do now is turn the key and the portal door should open," Bash said.

Kam pushed Bash out of the way and turned the key himself. The blue circle turned into a door they could physically walk through, like the one they had first fallen through when they arrived in Pollutio.

"I can see the castle!" Kai said excitedly.

The four of them smiled at each other then slowly stopped until their smiles turned upside down.

"Thank you, guys, for teaching me and Kam how to be better friends and how to truly understand what it's like to be a normal human that has feelings,"

Kam said. "Now we can be better leaders to our people of Aeolus."

"Yes, thank you for being great friends," Kai said.

Kai and Kam bowed to Mira and Bash, but Bash stopped them.

He said, "No, thank you for forgiving me, even though I betrayed you."

Bash bowed lower than the twins had to show them even more respect. Mira followed his lead and bowed on the ground beside Bash.

"Come visit us, okay? With your portals or something." Mira tried to laugh to keep the twins from seeing the tear rolling down her face.

Mirroring Mira, the twins laughed, too, then stood to their feet. Mira and Bash gave Kai and Kam one last hug before they said their goodbyes.

"Farewell, our friends," Kai and Kam said in unison.

Home at last, the twins thought to each other, happy that their telepathy powers were back to working at full strength.

CHAPTER 14

The twins were gone, and it was down to just two—Mira and Bash. They were as silent as a mouse as they looked around everywhere but at each other. Still uncomfortable, Bash spoke first.

"Mira, I know it has been very rough here, and I'm sorry you got caught by the monster because of me..."

Mira turned her face away from Bash. He stopped speaking as she made little gasps. Bash shuffled to see her face. When he did, he realized she was crying.

"I'm really sorry. I didn't mean to make you upset," Bash said, tripping over his words as they came out of his mouth.

"Bash, I'm not mad at you. I'm sad that I have to leave you. I have to go back to my reality... that's hard for me." Mira said.

Bash reached out to give Mira a hug. "Don't worry. You can visit me anytime you want to because now we know how the portal works," he said. "You are welcome to come to Pollutio anytime." Bash smiled as big as the sun.

"Thank you, Bash. This was a very great experience, and I will be coming back."

Mira and Bash said their last goodbyes, then Bash used the book to open the portal back to Earth for Mira.

"Bye, Bash! See you later," Mira yelled after stepping inside.

She didn't hear if Bash said anything back to her. Mira was back on Earth and in the same place she was before she had left—on the field trip in the gardens of the Cummer Museum. Mira headed back toward her group that she had run from before.

"It's Mira, guys! She's back!" one classmate yelled.

The group came running toward Mira.

"Mira, we were so scared! We were looking for you everywhere. Are you okay?" another classmate asked.

Mira, feeling guilty, tried to hold back her tears. "I'm sorry, guys. I was being very selfish and bratty and not caring about everyone's opinions. I feel bad. I'm sorry."

A single tear ran down Mira's face. Her classmates surrounded her even more and tried to comfort her with their closeness.

"It's okay, Mira. We were more worried about you than what happened earlier," one said.

"Don't worry about it. It's all in the past," another classmate stated.

Mira wiped her face and smiled. "Thank you, guys, for being my classmates. Let's make the rest of this trip a good one."

Mira walked back toward the gardens with her friends to enjoy the rest of their trip, finally understanding why it was so important to listen to others.

Acknowledgements

Jacksonville Arts & Music School (JAMS) is a creative arts and youth leadership focused after-school program whose mission is to empower the creative leaders of tomorrow. Special thank you to the students of House Savage, our visual arts department named in honor of Augusta Savage; Director of Education & Visual Art Instructor, Erin Kendrick; JAMS Writer-in-Residence and publisher, Nikesha Elise Williams; and The Cummer Museum of Art & Gardens Education, Gardens, and Marketing Staff.

Kim Kuta Dring, Director of Learning & Engagement
Patrick MacRae, Director of Gardens & Horticulture
Dulcie Hause, Asst. Director of Learning & Engagement
Karl Boecklen, Adult Programs Manager
Dima Kroma, Youth & Family Programs Manager
Craig Whitlock, Graphic Designer & Marketing Specialist

www.ingramcontent.com/pod-product-compliance
Lightning Source LLC
Chambersburg PA
CBHW070539310726
48982CB00010B/1409/J
* 9 7 8 1 7 3 5 7 2 1 9 6 5 *

The Cathode Ray Chronicles: Bright Future

Ben Trandem

Cover art by Joe Dressel

Interior art by Ben Trandem

For Connie, Ada and Zoe. My constant constellations.

Special Thanks to my personal editor and best friend Lance.

Contents

PROLOGUE

89%

Cathode feels like the data transmission rate has been moving at a horrible crawl the entire time.

No way should they get closer. Safer distance is better.

Looking up from the control panel all she can see through the ship's front display is the burning white light of the sun. Even filtered down to barely a hundredth of it's true strength it still makes her tired eyes hurt.

Long day.

Cathode smirks to herself as her gaze turns away from the sun. Off to the left she sees a sparkle that is Venus among the stars. Using her gloved hand to shield her eyes through her helmet's visor she looks back down to the pilot control panel.

97%

Her hand floats over the throttle control. Even with her helmet on, the loud sound of the air leaking out of his suit catches her off guard. Lazy has climbed out of the cargo hold and painfully strapped himself down in the co-pilot seat. He gives a weak thumbs up with his left hand reiterating they were successful.

Looking past Lazy's left hand to his suit's abdomen area Cathode can see the air escaping from between his fingers. Even with his hand pressed firmly against his stomach he can't make it airtight. The escaping air takes large stringy beads of blood with it. His hand slips slightly letting out a hard whine of air and more floating blood particles. She forces her eyes to stay clear

No. She thinks to herself.

Lazy sees her face contort and tries to make his goofiest smile possible. It comes off as a far more pained expression than he intended but the effect is the same. She weakly smiles back at him.

100%

The console chimes as their data files complete their transfer.

"OK. It's sent," Cathode says.

Her voice wavers as she speaks into the ship's communication system.

Crackling slightly through the speakers of the cockpit her voice echoes back

"OK. Received."

She wants to say something. Get something out that might be a bit more profound at a time like this. She opens her mouth as if to make her big final speech but pauses. Cathode knows the most important information has passed on in those data files. Her gaze falls on a greeting card wedged into the driver side dashboard. It's a drawing of a cup of noodles and the card is cut into the shape of the cup with a pair of chopsticks sticking out of the partially opened top. Sighing, she turns off the ship's communications.

Cathode unbuckles from the pilot seat and her weightless body floats up slightly. She maneuvers herself over to the co-pilot seat and gently lowers herself onto the dash in front of Lazy's seat. She puts a foot on his knee to steady herself. Even though Cathode is currently weightless he makes a pained face as if she was crushing him. She almost laughs. Her smile stretches harshly back across her face as she begins to cry. Cathode leans her head forward so she is pressed visor to visor with Lazy. She looks into his eyes with hazy vision. He smiles back at her through pale lips. With her free right hand she reaches out to grab the throttle control. She says one last thing.

"Bye... Again."

She taps the throttle control down. She can see his mouth moving. Lazy is saying "bye" back to her but she can't hear him. The control panel reads a decrease in throttle of .5%. The bomb they had been keeping pace with, the one currently floating, primed by Cathode, in the cargo hold, seems to lurch forward even though it is actually their ship that is slowing down. Lazy wraps both of his hands around Cathode's left, letting oxygen and blood expel freely. She puts her right hand on Lazy's visor as the bomb strikes the front of the cargo hold.

Out of the corner of her eye, behind Lazy's helmet, Cathode can see a second blinding white sun expanding toward her for the briefest of moments. She, Lazy and the ship are consumed in pure white energy for the second time.

Her head, ever so slowly, tips forward further and further. Just before her chin is about to touch her collar her head snaps back up. This is the third time, in this class alone, Catherine Rei has started to nod off. She rubs the sleep from her eyes and looks around the high school classroom. No one seems to have noticed her. As usual. Who would? Being, as she thought, an average looking, if somewhat frumpishly dressed, sixteen year old girl. Constantly wearing layered t-shirts and overly baggy tan construction pants. Always sitting in the back of classes. Never speaking up. She was quite well known for being reprimanded and suspended for various academic violation reasons. She figured she wasn't, nor would ever be, exactly Miss Popularity prom queen material. Or even someone most people would have a second thought about.

As recently as last semester she had been put on suspension for wearing a small decorative top hat to classes. Hats were not restricted from the classrooms at Aristarchus' Second High School. At least not at that point. But, installing a micro CPU capable of registering speech, scanning text on test sheets, searching the exter-net for the answers and then relaying them back using a digital speech program into an ear-bud was. She had only been caught when the "Magic Hat", as she nicked it, had lost exter-net signal and tried to reconnect automatically through the strongest available wireless network, the school's. Her teacher was informed, on her desk display mid-test, that someone in the school was searching for the exact words she had just spoken as part of the test's verbal section. It wasn't difficult for Catherine's teacher to deduce who it was.

Considering the network sniffing program that caught her was the same one that was installed colony wide in all the schools, although a few generations improved she noted, from when she used her goggles in junior high school to watch videos from the archives she should have been able to avoid detection. She kicked herself for leaving auto-reconnect on.

Amateur hour, Cathode. Might as well re-nick it the 'dunce cap' now.

It wasn't as though she needed to cheat in the first place. She had already correctly answered the entire test before her CPU hat could feed her the answers. It was simply that she could make the system work. Never that she should. She already wasn't very popular with much of the student body since they couldn't use their goggle systems on campus and now, also thanks to her, they couldn't even wear plain hats outside of gym and sports clubs.

She quietly yawned and stretched in her seat. Her desk screen was empty. She hadn't kept any notes and wasn't entirely sure what period she was now in. Possibly math. At a glance it seemed to be a lot of math type things written up on the board. She could be wrong. She could be in Japanese class. Her eyes almost immediately get heavy again. She tries to stay awake by doodling on the desk screen's notepad with her stylus. A few crude doodles and some random code lines she might save. The stylus slides across the screen leaving a large black digital line on the notepad application. She's falling asleep and again hoping people continue not to notice.

He notices. He always notices her in class. Having been Catherine Rei AKA Cathode Ray's best friend since elementary school Bradley Connelly AKA Buster Chaplin AKA Lazy Beam always knew when she was nodding off. He had changed his name, not legally, not yet, maybe later, when he had found an old directory of black and white videos on some archival exter-net servers. He had determined the videos were absolutely ancient since they had no dialog, strange word card things, and maybe a piano, if anything, playing as the soundtrack. Even so he found them immensely entertaining. Cathode had teased him for months when she found out where the names had come from. To rub it in she would call him Harold Keaton or Buster Barrymore. Thinking he could win, or at least redirect her taunts, he had suggested he change his nick to something thermal like Galaxicon or Laser Diode. With that he had succeeded in redirecting her taunts but ended up with a new nick he could never escape. He was forever branded Lazy Beam.

Slowly, waiting for Mrs. Thorsson's attention to turn back to the digital whiteboard, he pulls out a small portable storage device in the shape of a pen/stylus combo. Running the micro sized cord from the bottom of the disguised drive down to his lap he plugs it into a tiny exposed circuit board. A blue LED on the circuit board blinks twice. Smirking, Lazy looks back over his shoulder at Cathode. She has slid further onto her desk. Her stylus pokes her in the cheek as she sleeps on the desk's screen.

"GOOOOOOOOOOOOD MORNING VIETNAM!"

Cathode bolts upright and almost falls completely out of her chair. Mrs. Thorsson pauses briefly as a few kids laugh at the flummoxed Catherine sprawled across her chair. She corrects herself in her seat and coughs quietly as if to apologize. The ear bud Lazy had fashioned and given her that morning, which looks like an oddly large and ornate earring, had been designed to receive a very specific radio wavelength frequency. His impromptu radio station continues airing a mix of audio samples he had undoubtedly scrounged up from some archive. His ArcArc's group had access to flops of media. She glares down at him anyway. When he notices he blushes and goes to unplug his miniature circuit board transceiver. She shakes her head ever so slightly and lets her glare change to a smile. He smiles back tapping the flesh colored ear bud, almost completely hidden in his left ear, he custom made for himself. Movie quotes and music tracks play over the class she's now fully awake for. Using a hotkey she cleans off her desk's notepad app and realizes she still has no actual notes for the class.

Is it Science?

She slides out her tablet computer from the shoulder bag by her feet. Booting it up she loads a similar notepad app.

Lazy looks back at Cathode again and she motions with her stylus to the empty screen on her tablet. He nods and places his own tablet next to his desk's screen. With a hand swipe motion, across the desk's screen toward his tablet, all of his notes copy and reappear exactly the same on both screens. Opening an app that looks like a cartoon word balloon he taps an icon of an old nineteen-sixties era television set on the top of his IM friends list. A pop-up appears asking if he wants to share his current audio recording as well. He taps yes and a status bar quickly shoots to one hundred percent. He leans back enjoying an audio clip of a crazy sounding man talking about cigarettes, gasoline and worlds of water.

On Cathode's tablet screen a pop-up appears with an icon of a nineteen-fifties styled sci-fi laser gun with a sad face on the handle. She clicks it and her notepad app is immediately filled with an exact copy of Lazy's notes. At the bottom of the note page is an audio waveform with a flashing red record circle. Everything Mrs. Thorsson has said is being recorded and streamed to her now as well. She sets the tablet down and tries to hold back laughter as the same crazy guy Lazy is listening to talks about his missing eyeball.

The bell chimes and students begin to file out of classrooms. Cathode keeps her eyes focused to the ground as she walks to her next class. The halls are spacious as there are no student lockers in the main halls. As most students carry a tablet and small book bags for the entire day the only places for storage are in the gym and sports club locker rooms. Even with all of the extra width of the halls a group of large senior boys intentionally bump past Cathode knocking her off balance. She tries to correct herself but ends up passing her momentum off into a petite, fashionably dressed girl walking next to her. The girl, Cathode's friend, Margaret Winn, stumbles and crashes into the wall near her. Her backpack falls to the ground spilling its contents across the hall. Cathode stops, flips off the group of jocks, and squats down to help Margaret collect her things.

"Sorry, Margaret. I didn't see those roidies coming. Really. I'm sorry."

"Don't worry about it, Catherine. I know. It's okay. I know nobody knowingly touches me."

Cathode can hear the sadness in Margaret's voice even though she's smiling as if it was a joke. As she stands to hand back the last of Margaret's things Cathode sees her cybernetic prosthetic right arm. It's a fully functioning neurologically linked appendage connected just below her shoulder. It's mostly shaped by plastic casings that are covered by a thin layer of flesh toned silicone. From a distance it looks almost natural. If only slightly paler than her normal skin tone. Even so Cathode knows that Margaret almost always wears long sleeves to hide it as much as possible. As was the case today as Margaret tugs down the sleeves of her baby blue hooded sweatshirt. Cathode walks with her down the hall but they don't speak to each other. Seeing the way they walk people would think they didn't even know each other let alone were actually good friends.

She will never forget, even if she wanted to, the day Margaret lost her arm. It was a little over a year ago when they were still in junior high school. Most people heard it second hand or remembered the news reports but Cathode had been there. They were on the last day of their spring break. Something that had never made sense to Cathode.

How do you have a spring break in a place with no seasonal or climate changes?

They had been in the Forest for most of the day swimming near a set of waterfalls with some other students. Cathode had worn a long white shirt over her one-piece swimsuit but Margaret had gone in a bikini. Cathode remembered being a bit jealous of how confident Margaret was with her body and how much attention she was getting from the other students. It didn't help when Margaret had said Cathode looked like a jellyfish when she was swimming in that shirt. Remembering that tinge of jealousy makes Cathode hate her own stinking guts just a little bit more for being that petty. Especially with what happened after they left the Forest.

The lift system they took down dropped them at Orion Station. Cathode had switched into a pair of shorts and had her towel wrapped around her neck like a scarf. Margaret had also put on shorts but had opted to remain in her bikini top as they waited for the next maglev-rail to arrive. Cathode could smell the alcohol on his breath before she even saw him. A college aged boy, she would never consider him a man, was stumbling up the steps from the street level to the platform. He yelled something to his departing friends before turning and slamming into a maglev-rail gate system as it auto-closed on him. He fumbled with his wallet, pulling out a pass card and swiped it over the gate system's reader before staggering forward. Cathode watched him like spectators viewed gorillas at the zoo; an intense interest in the spectacle but a twinge of fear at what could happen if the beast were let loose to approach you. Cathode finally turned away when he stepped up behind them and belched. It made Margaret giggle but she was also distracted by a message on her Personal Mobile Device. Cathode could then smell and feel his nasty breath on her back. The drunkard slowly side-stepped around them so he could look them in face.

"Hey. You ladies enjoying your spring break?"

Cathode looked through him. Margaret looked up for a brief moment with a polite smile before returning to taping out a message on her PMD.

"Gettin' your swim on, yeah?"

He reached out attempting to snap the upper strap of Margaret's bikini. As his fingers had just barely reached their destination Cathode realized his intentions and leapt forward shoving him away.

"Don't you touch her!"

Other people waiting for the train had turned to see why a small girl was yelling and shoving a grown man to the ground while her even smaller friend was covering her chest. Some of them pulled out their PMDs and began recording videos. Cathode grabbed onto Margaret's arm and started to walk her further down the platform. The drunk picked himself up and charged after her. Cathode wasn't looking back so it came as quite a shock when the drunk shoved her square in the back. Her grip slipped from Margaret's arm and she fell, sliding a few feet across the dirty platform surface. The drunk wasn't finished. He stomped over and kicked Cathode in the stomach while screaming in her face.

"What's your problem?! You think you can just push people around?"

He kicked into Cathode again. She coughed and began dry heaving. Just as he was lining up to kick again Margaret reached out for his shoulder. That was the scene that would be replayed ad-nauseam for the next two months on the news feeds. All from different angles of peoples PMDs and the platform's security system. The drunk spun around hooking his hand under Margaret's left armpit and lifting her up off her feet. Twisting, the drunk threw her sideways toward the maglev-rail. Had she not grabbed his shirt at the last second she would have fallen into the track path. Instead he was carried along with her. She hit the ground hard and he fell on top of her. Cathode was able to look up just as the maglev-rail floated into the station. The drunk's momentum caused him to roll over Margaret's body and onto the central rail as he dragged her right arm into the path of the arriving maglev-rail train. Both he and Margaret's arm were gone in a blurry instant. Cathode forced herself to her knees. Then popped up to her feet and ran to Margaret. Cathode dragged her away from the stopped train and wrapped Margaret's right shoulder with her beach towel. Cathode didn't know what to say to her. She did the only thing she could think of that would be useful. She knelt and put all her weight onto Margaret's shoulder to slow the bleeding. In her mind there was no sound but she could see Margaret screaming. Margaret swatted with her left arm for Cathode to move but she remained planted as blood soaked the towel. Looking up Cathode could see the long red stain across the side of the train. When she turned her head to look around all the noise flooded in as she saw people still standing around recording them with their PMDs. She screamed at them.

"Call an ambulance!"

She learned later that several people already had but from her vantage point she only saw the gawkers. She held Margaret's hand the rest of the time. All the way from the platform, to the ambulance, and finally to the hospital. She even stayed in Margaret's room after surgery. All she could do was blame herself for inciting the incident. They couldn't reconnect Margaret's arm because there frankly wasn't enough of it left after the accident. They even had to use the video feeds to identify the college boy because of how mangled the limited remains of his body had become.

A few weeks later Margaret was fitted with her prosthetic. Cathode had gone every day to help her with the physical therapy. Once Margaret had gotten control of the arm Cathode hacked the firmware so Margaret could at any time, if she wanted, increase her arm's strength by around four times its normal output.

It was around this time Cathode started nicking Margaret as Manticore. As if she was slowly becoming a mythical creature made up of stronger and stronger parts. She wasn't sure exactly why but it seemed to make Margaret smile so she kept using it. They hadn't really talked all that often after Margaret was released from the hospital. Cathode had a sinking feeling that Margaret's parents had read up on Cathode's academic problems after the accident and forced Margaret to cut off ties with her. Sometimes she would receive a random instant message from Manticore just wanting to talk but almost never from Margaret in person. Unless it was strictly school related.

As they head toward the exit of the school Cathode keeps slightly parting her lips on the verge of saying something before snapping her jaw shut. She looks at Margaret who is staring at the ground. A rage boils in her that she can't even just say something, anything at all, at the right time. It's as if someone jammed an inhibitor chip in her skull just so she'd look like an insensitive freak. Margaret continues her solemn walk as Cathode stops to pull out her tablet. She taps in a few quick lines of code and sends an instant message to an icon that looks like a red Egyptian sphinx. Margaret's head perks up as a faint buzzing noise is heard. She looks down at her hoodie's pockets perplexed. Margaret slides her PMD awkwardly out of her right pocket with her left hand. She still doesn't fully trust her prosthetic when handling delicate things. She opens the message and sees an animation of a swimming jellyfish waving at her. Just as she exits the school she looks back at Cathode who is trying to smile sheepishly. Margaret smiles warmly back and files out of the school with the rest of the student body. Replacing her tablet in her bag Cathode pivots on her feet and swings her arm out. She connects, punching Lazy in the stomach playfully. He play acts, selling the punch, as if it knocked the wind out of him, crumpling to his knees. He raises a fist to the sky.

"Why?!"

He clenches his stomach and waves his hand sickly in Cathode's face. She swats it away with a loud smack.

"You were following me."

"I wasn't following you. I'm headed to the exit. That thing over there. And then I'll just happen to be walking in the same general direction as you. Since we've lived in the same neighborhood our whole miserable dull lives. Ya spazzoid."

Cathode reaches out and grips Lazy's ear in her hand. He winces as she is actually applying pressure this time.

"A likely story. Who sent you?! Was it the Zoanoids?!"

A few students pass unimpressed by the weird theater kids amateur theatrics. Lazy stands upright, also bored with the play acting.

"You sure are cranky when you don't get your fourteen hours of sleep."

She slaps his stomach again, with a bit more force, and walks out of the school doors with him.

"*Somebody* decided to keep me awake in class."

"*Somebody* shouldn't have to keep you awake but you also don't need any more reprimands from the administration. How's Manticore doing? Pretty sure her parents do not like me anymore. Not that I believe they ever really did."

"Seems the same. Maybe after the end of the semester we can convince her to do a day trip somewhere."

Cathodes gently pushes Lazy out of the way as a small group of girls seem to skip past. Under her breath Cathode whispers to Lazy.

"Watch out for the floaters."

Lazy stifles a laugh as he catches sight of the girls. Cathode had shared a video with him a few nights ago in which a late night talk show host described the new teen fashion of wearing lighter weight terran clothes to seemingly float around as you moved on Luna. And how he, or his writers, had finally cracked it. Gave it a name. The swanky models flaunting this new fashion style would be known as "floaters".

The group of girls pay them no attention as they trot out of the school. Exiting the school's main building Cathode looks up. It's a very bright day out. Everything is lit as if it were roughly high noon. The sky looks cloudy, like it will rain, though. A large group of students jog by, just starting to warm up for their sports club activities. They weave around Cathode and Lazy who are just trying to make it to the front gates as fast as possible. Cathode tilts her view to the southwest, her orientation method for the city, to see the seam of the sky box where its edge partially overlaps. She's seen these clouds before, about a month ago.

Someone should update the feeds with new videos.

Lazy and Cathode slip on their goggles for the walk home. Students on benches just outside the school grounds are slipping on their hats and goggles. A few glare at Cathode as she passes before closing the black-out irises on their goggles. She disregards them by holding her gaze to the sky.

The sky box is the video feed that plays around the entire fake roof of the colony's City level. The side walls, about ten stories up, all the way to the pinnacle opening of the ceiling, are made up of networked video feeds to make the City seem like it has a real Earth sky. At the pinnacle is a wide circular opening about a quarter of the diameter of the entire city. This massive opening is where all the natural sunlight, once it's filtered down through the Forest level, is mirrored out around the domed ceiling and walls. The mirrors create a ring around the opening and slowly change their angles during the day to keep a realistic feel to the amount of light seeping in depending on the time of day.

In between the Forest and City levels is the parking storage for vehicles and major equipment. It also has a halo of mirrors spreading light across its massive area. Storage's mirrors don't move though as it just keeps a standard base level of illumination at all times. Also on Storage is a large underground tram system that links the Aristarchus city to three other nearby lunar colonies. There is construction already underway for two more lines to connect the entire Oceanus Procellarum area. Storage is the only level with publicly accessible airlock gates. Rovers, cycles, buses, trucks, small hovercrafts and other vehicles all come in through 3 different gates around the edge of the crater.

The Forest area is on top of all major colony structures and acts, mainly, as a combination oxygen plant and sun filter. The water in the Forest is filtered up through the top transparent barrier of the crater where it is evaporated by filtered light and then forced back down the sides to create the waterfalls. The waterfalls feed rivers that lead into the central lake. The lake is the second filter and its transparent bottom is where all light travels through to reach the Storage and City levels. The water from the lake is eventually funneled into an electric dam system that pipes it back up to the top barrier to create an endless filtration loop. The exteriors of the crater colony systems are a cap of solar panels that extend from the surface of the moon to the transparent Forest barriers. From above, the black solar paneling makes the crater appear to be concave instead of convex. There are roughly eighty crater colonies on the moon with Aristarchus being one of the oldest. Although it is no longer the biggest. Its population dwindled for a generation as several newer colonies opened up but has been on the rebound recently.

Cathode pushes Lazy playfully away from her as they reach a public park that separates rows of old block apartment buildings. Lazy waves over his shoulder and heads off to a tan six story apartment complex across the street from the park. Cathode walks through the park's playground equipment toward a reddish brick eight story apartment building behind it. She has her goggles set on a low transparency level so she can view a video as she walks. The goggles' heads up display makes the video seem like it is roughly five feet in front of her. The HUD also registers and outlines any objects in her immediate path in red. She doesn't notice the red bouncy rocket spring rider, for what seems like the hundredth time, and stubs her toe on its large spring base. She curses under her breath before tapping the side of her goggles. The video pauses and fades away. An audio recording app appears hovering in its place.

"Adjustment note. Patch collision immediacy program so red objects are outlined in a different color. And! Actually do it this time. Don't delete this until the patch is complete, future me."

Tapping the side of her goggles again the recording app states it is saving a copy of the newly created file to her tablet and fades away. The video reappears but Cathode doesn't start it. She steps into the main doorway of the eight story apartment building. Her family's dwelling since she can remember. Stepping up to the security door she pulls out a flat metal card and slides it into a security slot next to the door. The door buzzes and then pings with recognition freeing the lock. She swings open the heavy door and pockets her apartment key.

Why would anyone need security like this in a controlled and sealed dome? It's not like they wouldn't be able to find a burglar, murderer or crazy within the full list of citizens saved on the archives. You can't get in or out without a passcard and you're on some form of camera ninety percent of the time, she routinely thought.

Shifting her shoulder bag she begins playing the video from where she left off. She rides the elevator to the seventh floor and exits to a tiny hallway with two doors and a single light. Apartments 7A to her left and 7B to her right. She heads left, and using her metal keycard again, slides into her family's apartment.

The Rei family apartment is quite spacious as it takes up half of the floor space of the seventh floor. Her dad had purchased it when Catherine's mother was pregnant with her younger brother, Mikko. It has a full kitchen, living room, master bedroom, two smaller bedrooms, two full baths and a laundry closet. The two smaller bedrooms were connected to the full bath and mirrored nearly identically. Still Cathode likes to believe she got the bigger room. She kicks off her shoes in the lowered entranceway and slides out her slippers from a shoe rack to her right. She knew her mom wasn't home from work yet as her slippers would have been out and waiting for her. She walks without lifting her feet, sliding across the imitation wood floors in between the kitchen, to her left, and living room, to her right. Dropping her shoulder bag behind the living room's couch she stops to yawn and stretch a bit. Sliding up to the first bedroom door she peeks into her brother's bedroom. She doesn't hear any noise from inside.

He must be at club practice today. What club did he join again?

Mikko had just started junior high school and was completely gung-ho about staying late to practice with his new club teammates. Cathode never really paid attention to him when he talked about it, or most things, so she still wasn't sure what club he was in.

Possibly a sport? Probably a sport. Am I a bad sister?...Probably.

A faintly nasally robotic voice calling out to her snaps Cathode out of her mildly depressing thought

"Huan ying hui jia, Master Cathode. Beam Queen of the Cubes Gleamed."

On her bed a medium sized teddy bear has come to life and is attempting to stay standing while maintaining a formal bow. Gizmoto, as she named him, is a simple bipedal robot kit she had re-purposed and covered with the fur "skin" of her favorite childhood teddy. She had added motion sensors to his camera eyes, a full vocal box, and a much larger animation kit to his database for him to act out. Her favorite thing to do was program him with amusing death scenes from archive videos. So much so she asked Lazy to clip any good ones he gets from his ArcArc group.

Gizmoto corrects his posture and stands staring at Cathode with big black soulless button eyes that hide his advanced motion sensor cameras. She smirks. He scratches his ear as a sign he is in one of his idle animations.

"Cowboys."

Gizmoto squeals as he comes to life. His arms grab for his belly and he stumbles backward as if shot. Making pained noises with each little step he inches to the edge of the bed.

"Argh... ya got me, pardner!"

Raising his paws above his head Gizmoto dives off the bed to the floor. He bounces off a pile of clothes and lands on the floor frozen in his dive stance.

"Gizmoto. Hibernate."

Gizmoto acts as if he's stretching his muscles and curls into a ball at the edge of the large pile of clothes. He makes a few noises like a purring cat before going into his silent hibernation state.

Cathode belly flops onto her now vacated bed as she enters her bedroom. The video she's been watching finishes and she closes it revealing a long list of links. Lazy always updated his "UMustC" video links each week. She had always marveled at the sheer amount of content he linked to. Especially considering that what she saw was only what he deemed good enough to share with her and a select group of mutual friends. She was almost certain he had to be running multiple video windows at the same time most nights. That was before she learned of the Archives Archaeologist group he was a part of helped cultivate his own server and the list. She was grateful for it even if she often made jokes about how the group sounded like a sea lion call. Whenever Lazy brought up the group she'd straighten her arms out and clap them together.

"Arc! Arc! What's new? Arc! Arc! Feed me fish!"

I'm a jerk. Maybe a funny jerk. But still a jerk.

She clicks a tiny icon that looks like a thumbs up next to the video she has just watched on the link list. ChoushinseiFlashman.s01e08.mp4 is highlighted in neon green before fading off the list. All items on the list slide up one slot in a stuttered animation. Cathode rolls over on her bed and clicks the next link TheMaxx.s01e01.avi. A new video window appears and begins playing a short animated program.

Cathode's room is decorated rather sparsely. Besides her bed, dresser, bookcase, bedside table and desk there is only a few personal effects. On her walls are digital picture frames featuring random movie and TV show posters to videos she had seen off Lazy's list. She learned that posters were used to sell videos back when they played at a thing called a theater. Currently, the posters were from a few different romantic movies of people kissing in the rain. Lazy had found them boring or annoying but she found herself really enjoying them. They were also the only thing she considered girly in her room. Even though her furniture was a mix of pinks and purples. She never felt like repainting since she'd had them since her family had first moved in. Her bookcase was filled with coding manuals for several languages, mangas, graphic novels, and old paperback novels her mother had kept from when she was a child. No romance novels, plastic dolls or sticker books. Her desk was covered in small electronic pieces, a purple soldering gun with pink glitter flowers adorning the grip, piles of open manuals, and a single pink unicorn riding across a rainbow bridge lamp. So, the solder gun was the second girliest thing in her room. The unicorn lamp was the last present she can remember her dad actually giving to her in person for her birthday. She was nine when he had given her the lamp. Since then, he had sent or ordered things depending on where he was during the years. Clothes covered a good eighty percent of the rest of her room. Even with a full sized closet and large dresser she never seemed to see more of her floor.

Rolling over onto her back Cathode enjoys the end credits of her new video as she wraps herself in her crumpled bedspread and yawns very wide. A tiny red timer flashes in the top right corner of her goggles' vision. She throws off her bedspread in a huff and sits up. She peels off the black and pink shirts she wore to school, careful to not disturb her goggles, and drops them to the floor. Digging in a pile of clothes near the foot of her bed she pulls out a dark green polo shirt. Yanking the shirt out of the pile causes hibernating Gizmoto to go rolling under her desk. She slides the shirt over her head with the same care not to bump her viewing experience. The logo on the polo shirt reads "Ultra Mega Foods". She also changes into a dark pair of khaki pants and lumbers out of her bedroom. Stopping at the refrigerator she takes out an energy soda and a protein enriched snack bar. She opens the snack bar, folds it in half and pops the entire thing into her mouth. She smacks at it loudly and cracks open the soda. She slurps from it while still chewing on the snack bar. Walking to the front door she picks up her shoulder bag. While biting down onto the soda can's lip she uses both hands to tuck in her work shirt. She switches into her outdoor shoes and walks out the door.

Tossing the empty energy soda can into a recycling bin next to a maglev-rail platform vending machine Cathode eyes another soda but decides against it. She turns around and waits for her train to arrive. Near the vending machines a small group of three people are loudly singing a hymnal song Cathode is unfamiliar with. She peeks back at them as they pass out flyers for their religious group. Passing commuters walk by trying not to make eye contact. All three of the religious group are wearing the same outfit; A light green tracksuit with giant circular patches on the sleeves and back of some sort of solar arrangement with a big emphasis on the sun at the center. They also have the same haircut. Even the woman in the group. It's a tri-hawk with three rows of hair that connect at a circle on the back of the head like rays of the sun lining their pale skulls. They also have white crystal LEDs stuck to their foreheads. Or, at least the younger man has it glued to his forehead. The older man and the woman both appear to have fully implanted crystal LEDs. Cathode smirks at the silly haircuts. The older man in the group catches her smirking and walks over with a frighteningly large smile. She doesn't have time to react as his arm shoots out and holds a pamphlet a few inches from her face.

"Here you are, little sister."

Cathode can't pretend she doesn't see him so she meekly takes the pamphlet from his hand and nods. Somehow his smile seems to expand even more as he returns to his group. Cathode looks around and realizes the only trash near her is right behind the religious group next to the vending machines. She loosely crumples the pamphlet and shoves it into her shoulder bag. She stares straight ahead, across the mono-track, hoping Mr. Smiles back there doesn't come back. She tries to focus her thoughts on something else. The stations seem a bit uglier with the addition of the "accident prevention shields". They are big four foot gray automated doors installed in front of the railways that only open when the train has arrived and fully stopped. Cathode wasn't sure which made her more uneasy; the fact they had them installed at every station after Margaret's accident or that they weren't part of the design in the first place. They had blamed a sharp increase in suicides a few weeks after the accident but Cathode knew it wasn't because of some made up statistic. If someone wanted to go out that way they didn't really need any fancy parkour skills to get over the barriers. Plus, it wasn't like living in a crater on the moon was the safest place in general. Just rent a rover, take it out a few yards, step out, remove helmet and kiss the astroturf goodbye.

Oh, hello again dark thoughts... go away.

She really needed to stop watching so many of the horror videos Lazy was sending her. It was making her overly morbid. As she has that thought she brings up Lazy's video link doc and adjusts the ranking system to force anything with the metadata labels like horror, terror, vile, morbid, grotesque and disgusting to the bottom of the list. She hovers over "thriller" and decides to leave it. The list updates and closes as her train floats into the station. It stops and as its doors open the AP shields spring to life, opening with flashing security lights. She shuffles in with a few haggard looking office workers and sits down next to the opposite side's door. She plays another video as the train pulls away from the station. Just as the video starts Mr. Smiles of the religious group catches her attention and waves at her while still singing. Returning his gaze, with a deranged smile of her own, Cathode shuts the black-out irises on her goggles.

Exiting the train at the Gunderson Street station Cathode taps her goggles. The irises for the display screens open. She blinks, allowing her eyes to adjust to not looking through tinted glass. She slides the goggles up over her head and stuffs them into her bag. She passes through the station gates and heads to Ultra Mega Foods grocery store a few blocks down the street. As Cathode enters her manager, Jeremy, is dealing with a complaining customer. She slinks, like a ninja she believes, behind the confrontation and into the employee break room. Depositing her bag in a locker with the initials C.R. she shuts the door and runs her finger across the biometric locking system. She runs her hands over her head to pull her hair into a ponytail.

"Catherine!"

Cathode jumps as Jeremy shouts her name behind her. She turns around to see his fuming face a few feet from her.

"The customer is always right, right?"

Cathode smiles and raises her arms as if in defeat. Jeremy doesn't seem amused. He's a tall, skinny man in his late twenties but the stress of his job apparently has aged him, at least in Cathode's mind, another ten. He even has tiny gray streaks of hair coming in across his temples. His face remains taunt, not helping him look younger.

"Miguel called in sick today. Again."

"Oh? Is that my fault?"

Cathode's face quickly drops, realizing she just sassed her boss. His face lightens. She knows he tries to maintain a hard nosed appearance but is actually one of the kindest older persons she's ever had to deal with.

"You're saying you didn't pay him off so he'd call in sick? Just so you'd get to run external deliveries today?"

Cathode lets a giant smile overtake her face.

"Really? Ex-Delivs?"

Jeremy nods as he passes her and grabs a coffee mug out of a cupboard above the break room's small sink.

"If I'd know this was what would happen I sure would have tried to bribe him."

Jeremy shoots Cathode a look that says "Don't push it". He pours some coffee in his mug and takes a large drink from it. He makes a strange face and dumps the coffee into the sink. He painfully, slowly, swallows what is in his mouth.

"Get suited up. Don't forget your passcard. I don't want to have to ride the lifts all the way up to the gates just to tell them you are in fact who you say you are."

"Right. No problem boss. I'm on my way."

Cathode slides her finger across the biometric lock on her locker again to unlock it and opens the door. She pulls her employee passcard out of her bag and slips her goggles onto her head.

"And no watching videos while you're driving the rover."

Cathode takes in a breath through her nose but before she can open her mouth Jeremy cuts her off.

"Even if it's on auto-drive. You almost ripped out the rear suspension last time."

"If you'd just let me upgrade the auto-drive I wouldn't have-"

"No! No. Listen, I told you this before. It's not up to me. Company policy says you can't tinker with any of the equipment. Hardware or software. I think they even mention you by name in the training manual."

"Very funny."

"I'm not kidding."

"Really?"

Jeremy smirks while washing out his mug.

"OK, maybe I'm exaggerating about the name thing. But, you sure don't want to be as notorious in lunar corporations as you are in the school system, right?"

Cathode reaches for the break room door.

"True."

Jeremy crouches down to find coffee filters beneath the coffee maker.

Cathode leaves the breakroom and heads to the back of the store avoiding as many customers as she can. Being on delivery is probably the best job at her work if not of any job she could think of in the crater. Freedom, alone time, and the chance to actually use the driver's license she had gotten eight months ago. At the loading dock door she enters and takes a medium sized green tinted space suit out of its security locker. She slips into the jumpsuit and seals it to her neck. It auto resizes to her body using a built in compression system. Sliding down her goggles she taps them so the display irises close and runs a system check on the suit. The last person to wear it apparently fell and scraped off part of the right knee. The entire legging was replaced with a newer darker green design giving the entire suit an awkward hodgepodge appearance. But, it's at a hundred percent, which is more important than fashion sense once you are outside the crater on the surface. Taking the helmet under her arm she walks down a low set of steps past the truck delivery port to the docking prep area for the exterior rovers.

A big robotic arm swings toward the rover as she approaches. It holds a massive long white rectangular drawer in its claw hand. The arm adjusts and lines up the drawer with the last remaining open slot on the back of the rover. It slowly slides the drawer in until a clicking noise is heard and a small green light flashes on just above the drawer. The claw releases and the arm swings up and away to its rest position. The delivery rover resembles a box truck buggy with oversized tires and a large white square refrigerator unit containing eight large drawers, four on each side, on its bed.

On Cathode's goggles a manifest appears with the list of delivery sites. Of the eight container drawers only five have green lights on. Each listed for one of three addresses on her delivery sheet. Her estimated travel time of three hours flashes on the bottom of the manifest. With her right hand she lowers her ring and pinky fingers, presses her thumb against her pointer finger and swipes across the estimated travel time. The three is highlighted. She writes in the air a number five. Then, a window pops up asking her if she really wants to make that change. She taps "yes" out of the air in front of her. A warning appears stating she will need approval before changes are saved. Sliding into the rover's cab enclosure she sets her helmet on the passenger seat and taps the main button on a small control box situated on top of the dash. The large metal gate behind her raises up. She pushes the ignition button next to the rover's steering wheel. The vehicle powers on almost silently and the center of the dash blinks on, displaying on its large screen, a copy of her manifest. Since the grocery refrigerator container blocks her vision she turns on the rear view camera system on the dash display screen. It flickers to life and shows her a fish eye view off the tailgate of the rover. Slowly, she backs the rover out, proceeding carefully into the side street behind the grocery store.

"Catherine, stop!"

She slams on the brakes. Which doesn't do much as she was moving very slowly to begin with. A small video appears on the dash display over the top of the rear view video window. Jeremy is looking sternly at her from a video camera feed on his office's desktop.

"One sec."

She resumes backing out and parks on the curb behind the store. Cathode throws the rover into park and lifts her goggles so Jeremy can see she is looking at his video window.

"What happened? Did I miss an order?"

"No. What's with the two hour addition? Planning to take a joy ride?"

Jeremy smirks at her.

"Because, I can tell you that is definitely not the vehicle you want to use for it."

"It's going to take me that long to make the deliveries."

"How do-"

"If I'm going to the northern mining outpost, as it says, then I'm going to need an extra hour both ways."

"For what?"

"They shut down the M-I-fifteen route because they're digging out the new tram system under it."

Jeremy blinks a few times before pressing his fingers to the bridge of his nose. He nods from behind his hand and taps a few keys on his keyboard.

"I wish they'd update the corporate nav maps more often. Lazy idiots..."

Even under his breath Cathode can hear Jeremy's mic. She doesn't react just in case. The manifest on Cathode's goggles updates with approval for the new time table.

"Anything else before I go?"

Jeremy sighs.

"Passcard?"

"Got it."

"Then, off you go."

The small video window closes as Jeremy disconnects. Cathode checks her side mirrors and external camera feeds before pulling out, headed toward the east side of the city.

After seventeen blocks she's come to the edge of the city and drives straight into an empty vehicle lift situated a few yards behind the city's wall. A large digital timer above the lift starts counting down from two minutes. She takes her time and carefully positions the rover on a large metal platter that is flush with the lift's floor. Even though she won't need to be turned around when she gets to Storage level she always tries to be a courteous driver. Especially when it's not her vehicle. Which is always.

Two more commuter cars zip onto the lift before the digital timer reaches zero and it shudders to life. Cathode is about to start a new video feed but she remembers Jeremy's warning and switches to her music player. She winces. She had set the volume too high while watching the previous, apparently horribly quiet, video and her music is blaring into her head. She quickly jogs the volume down to a suitable level and leans back. The lift takes an average of ten minutes to reach Storage so Cathode gets as comfortable as she can in the rover.

About halfway up, bored, she checks the manifest list again. Phalanx North Mining Outpost is on the top. Tapping the air brings up her map system with the M-I-fifteen crossed off. Her new route winds around Montes Harbinger and heads up to the tip of a gargantuan man-made hole in the ground that is the northern Phalanx mine. Estimated new time to destination is one hour fifty minutes. Second is the Meridian Oasis Port, a large fueling hub station with shopping and restaurants between the cities of Aristarchus and Herodotus. It is another destination that would have been faster to arrive at using the M-I-fifteen. And third is the Navitas Immensus Laboratories. Outside Cathode's own bedroom it is her favorite place in the entire galaxy. It is technically the closest to Aristarchus but she always saves it for last. Her actual entire travel time, according to her map system, is three hours fifty seven minutes. She knows it will only take roughly fifteen minutes to park and unload the delivery drawers at each location. That gives her a good half hour to spend at the Navitas Immensus Laboratories.

The lift reaches Storage level and stops with a slight bump. Cathode waits for the security gate to drop then drives forward. The two other vehicles on the lift begin to rotate on their platters back toward the roads into Storage. Roughly half a mile in front of her the tunnel's ceiling begins to gradually dip down until it connects with a large metallic gate system. It's flanked on either side by security booths. Two guards stand lazily by the left side talking about something as she approaches. Cathode stops the rover within a luminescent rectangle on the ground. She puts the rover in park and holds her passcard against the driver side window. One of the guards steps up and waves a scanner across her passcard. Her picture, information, weight and height of the vehicle, and destinations appear on the scanner's readout. He lethargically clicks a few buttons and nods to her. As he walks back to his post the other guard looks into the cab at Cathode. He taps his head at her. Cathode's brow wrinkles in confusion. The other guard waves his hand in front of his face. Cathode realizes she's not wearing her helmet yet. She smiles at him as she slides it on and twists it to seal it at her suit's collar. The lethargic guard steps into his booth and deposits the scanner into a cradle next to his CPU. He taps a few keys and the large metal gate in front of Cathode lets out a metallic grinding noise. The gate begins to split vertically at the center. Behind the first set of gates a second gate lifts from within the floor up toward the ceiling. Finally a second pair splits horizontally behind that with a heavy whoosh of escaping air. Cathode notices the other guard looks oddly relaxed, he is still standing outside the booth, as he slides a few inches sideways from the suction.

The gate doesn't open in its entirety however. It creates a square opening in front of Cathode a little over one and a half sizes of the rover. She cautiously pulls forward toward another projected luminescent rectangle inside the airlock chamber. She stops on it and the gates behind her close. A large display near the top of the gates in front of her states in neon red letters "Warning. De-compression in process. Please, do not exit your vehicle at this time." It flashes a few times for emphasis and remains on as the three gate system to the moon's exterior begins opening. It expands much larger than the first gate as a massive delivery truck is waiting on the outside to enter the crater. The gate expands to allow for them to pass each other safely. Cathode waves up at the cab even though she can't see inside of it. The massive truck honks its horn at her. Even though it seems childish it still makes her giggle. She turns left out onto a large gray paved street and heads toward an equally gray four-lane road. The Earth is high in the sky ahead of her and the sun is hanging low behind it.

"Volume up ten percent."

Her music volume smoothly rises as she begins her delivery trip.

Most of the workers at the Phalanx mine knew Cathode from when her dad was one of the mid-level foremen on the northern ridges. His "Take Your Daughter To Work" days had been a bit scary but also quite exciting for Cathode when she was much younger.

She takes the steps up two at a time. She taps the automated door handle and it slides away to let her enter a medium sized office building. There are offices dotting the exterior walls. In the center of the space is a small hive of about twenty cubicles filled with workers. Near the office doors and directly in front of the entrance are secretary desks. A few of the office workers greet her by name as she enters. The rover is in a bay below the office, two of its drawers being removed by similar robotic arms as the grocery store and placed into racks in the back of the office employee lunch hall. Cathode twists off her helmet and waves to the head secretary sitting at the largest of the desks. The stout Asiatic looking woman dressed in a bright business suit and heavy makeup waves back. Catherine beams at her.

"How is Mrs. Takigasaki?"

"Hello Catherine! I'm just fine dear. I don't know why I have to keep reminding you to just call me Miwa."

"Right. Well, I'm on the job right now, so I have to be business polite, ma'am."

Cathode slides a small tablet, with Ultra Mega Foods' logo emblazoned on the top of it, out of a plastic holster on her hip and slides it across Miwa's desk. On its screen is an itemized list of everything ordered by the Phalanx office staff from her manifest. It is updating in real time as, a few floors below them, administrative assistants in the lunch hall scan and remove the individual packages from inside the two drawers.

"You've become such a polite, responsible young lady, huh? How's your father doing at his new posting?"

Cathode takes a second to think of how she should answer that. She hasn't really heard from her dad in almost three months. She decides to lie and hide her concern for his safety.

"In the vid feed he sent a few weeks ago he said he's doing great. I think he's really enjoying being a foreman on his own site. 'Course he misses the family and the folks chipping away at this rock. And your strawberry mochi. Naturally."

Miwa smiles warmly at Cathode. The list on the small tablet finishes updating with a ping noise and flashes a signature box in a window that covers most of the screen.

"Are you sure it's your father who misses those? I seem to recall you have the sweet tooth for them."

Miwa wiggles her stylus playfully at Cathode. Cathode smirks back at her. She smiles with her teeth like a mischievous child.

"I mean, I wouldn't turn them down if you were offering."

Signing off on the order Miwa hands the tablet back to Cathode. She slides open a large drawer on her desk. Cathode slips the tablet back into its cradle on her suit's hip. Miwa pulls a large gift box out of the drawer. She flips off the top of the box revealing rows of soft rice candies in the shapes of fish and turtles. Having already unlocked it, Cathode twists off her right glove and daintily picks up one of the fish candies between her fingers.

"Oh, go on. Take two."

"Are you sure?"

"Of course."

"You suuuuuuuuure?"

Miwa grins at her and nods. Cathode quickly pops the fish in her mouth and picks up a turtle shaped candy. She tries to speak without spitting out the sticky sweet.

"Tanks, Miwa. Shee you nexsht time."

Miwa lets out a deep warm laugh and waves again as Cathode turns heading to the exit. Miwa places the box back in its drawer. Cathode taps the door handle and walks down the steps. She swallows and pops the turtle candy into her mouth. Pulling her glove out of her helmet she slides it on and seals it at the wrist. As she steps out of the elevator on the ground floor she turns to see both drawers have been returned to the rover's bed. She slides on her helmet and seals it with a heavy click.

"Mooshic. Blay."

An apathetic robotic female sounding voice asks from her goggles' earbuds, "Please, repeat command".

Swallowing the second candy Cathode repeats, "Music. Play."

Her music starts in the middle of the track she paused when she first entered the mining company offices. A few massive dump trucks pass by somewhere near the office area causing the earth to quake slightly. Cautiously, Cathode climbs into the rover's cab and waits for them to pass. When it seems all clear she pulls out and heads up a paved ramp leading toward an exit gate. The airlock gates of the mines always interested Cathode. They are set up in ramped steps of four gates. The offices are actually buried underground near the mine site for safety and to save on UV shielding costs because the company wants things as cheap as possible. At least that's what her dad told her. As she exits the fourth gate she pushes the rover's accelerator more than necessary. Coming from the gate's incline out to the flat road causes the rover to catch air for a brief second before landing with a rough bounce on the road.

And Jeremy thought I was watching videos last time. Ha!

Cathode sees the two gargantuan dump trucks that had caused the underground tremors pulling onto one of the roadways that leads deep down into the main mining area. She only briefly reconsiders doing her rover jump next time as the dump truck tires alone are roughly seven times the size of her little vehicle.

Maybe I'd be lucky and just get stuck inside a tread...

She drives toward an on-ramp for M-I-nine southbound. She passes a large graying billboard claiming the Meridian Oasis Port is only fifteen miles away. There is only light traffic of delivery vehicles and business commuters as she merges into a lane.

She doesn't know anyone who works at the Oasis and really doesn't care. The turnaround for the jobs in the area is quite heavy. High school and college kids make up the majority of the work staff with a small mix of housewives and elderly retirees who didn't want to leave, filling in the more permanent positions. She sits, sipping on a can of soda, waiting for two more drawers to be emptied and tagged in the distribution center next door. She has her goggles down and music on but she can still hear the conversation taking place behind her. Three guys all dressed in the same, Cathode thinks, ridiculous overalls outfit for the Oasis vehicle service shop are discussing how they plan to drive out onto the closed M-I-fifteen and drag race. She jogs her music up as they begin to argue who has the fastest, best looking, most modified machine. She jumps slightly as someone taps her on the shoulder. An awkward looking college aged boy in an unkempt gray dress shirt, loose black tie, and an assistant manager name tag is standing behind her holding the Ultra Mega Foods' branded tablet. She pauses her music and slides off her goggles.

"It said finished. Boss is out so I signed. Here."

The boy barely mumbles loud enough for Cathode to hear. She checks the screen.

"Tap 'Approved'."

The boy doesn't have a stylus on him so he taps the screen with his finger leaving a large oily fingerprint. Cathode sighs and takes it from him. He turns and shuffles off past the space racers who are still arguing loudly. Cathode tosses her can into the recycling bin and exits to the distribution center's garage. She almost starts skipping knowing her next destination. As she sits in the cab of the rover waiting for the last airlock gate to open out of the Oasis she actually claps her hands together lightly.

The quite nondescript facility was built on the edge of the Oceanus Procellarum lunar mare, semi-hidden in almost perpetual shadows. The site's position would be rather peculiar if it wasn't designed to be as hidden as possible. It's not necessarily a secret location as there are roads that lead to and from it. But, it is a government contracted science research and development facility that operates best in seclusion. Being carved into the side of the highest ridge of the Montes Carpatus mountain range helps further obscure its location and protect nearby colonies from any unfortunate accidents that might occur from within the facility. What branch of the government the facility is funded by falls under is "not known by the general public". Even Cathode has no real solid idea even though she's made deliveries there since she started her job at the grocery store. And, the only reason she can even make deliveries to the facility in the first place is due to her "in" with a higher level employee there.

Slowly, at a speed best described as "slower than a drunken snail", Cathode steers the delivery vehicle through the third security checkpoint. The first is a general scan, the second is a weight check, and the third is a deep MRI scan of the vehicle that requires the driver to "not stop" but also "do not exceed five miles per hour". This is all about half a mile out before you are even allowed to show a badge for entrance into the facilities airlock system. Cathode doesn't mind though. This is just the routine. She did try, just one time, to give the scanner system the finger. Whoever monitors the external checkpoints was not amused and forced her to back up and do it again like an adult. It pissed her off but now, having been to the facility several times, she understands the need for such strict safety measures. And it is serious so she should at least make an effort to also be serious about it. And she only does that because of how awesome the goodies are inside the facility.

After parking in the designated delivery spot, Cathode hops out of the cab as the automated delivery system's arms begin pulling the crates off the vehicle. She waves up at one of several cameras in the parking bay and walks with her order tablet into the main entrance. Gruffy McGrufferson is there to greet her as usual. Or, as his ID badge states he is "Brodin Mitchell, Head of Security, NAVITAS IMMENSUS LABORATORIES".

"Afternoon Mr. Mitchell, sir."

"Miss Rei. Did you make Miss Nelson aware of your delivery?"

"I mean, you're head of security, right? Doesn't it say there is a visitor badge just waiting for me?"

Cathode leans over the security desk to peek at Gruffy's screen. Without breaking eye contact with her Head of Security Brodin Mitchell presses his screen to pivot it ever so slightly away from her prying eyes. He sighs.

"I'll page her to come get you. Please, wait over there."

Head of Security Brodin Mitchell points to the only other chair in the room. A worn out metal torture device of a chair. Cathode stands, leaning on the security desk, for a moment before she walks over and heavily sits down in the chair making a loud clang combined with the chair legs scraping and screeching against the floor. She smiles politely at Gruffy McGrufferson the Gruffiest Gruffenstein who's ever gruffed. Without breaking off his stare at Cathode he taps a mic button on his desk.

"Paging Miss Nelson to security. Paging Miss Nelson to security."

He releases the button but does not move another muscle. Cathode, on the other hand, immediately begins fidgeting in her seat. She pulls off her goggles, her smart bracelet, several other small tech doodads from her pockets and piles them on her lap. As she finishes emptying her pockets the door behind the security desk opens with a groaning whoosh. Out steps a stunning, or as Cathode's preferred newly learned favorite slang term "a real corker", mid-thirties woman wearing a lab coat, her hair in a messy bun and little red dimples on the bridge of her nose from where she had just removed her safety goggles. Cathode notes this is the only time The Beast known as Gruff breaks eye contact with her to scope out the total science babe that just walked in. Ms. Nelson waves at Cathode with a beaming smile on her face.

"Catherine!"

Cathode stands up, dumps the contents of her lap into a bin on the edge of the security desk labeled "Unsecured Electronics", and loudly drops the delivery tablet in front of McGrufferooony. He's momentarily startled away from gawking at Ms. Nelson. Cathode grins at him.

"I'm gonna need that signed off on when I get back, McGruff."

A not amused Head of Security Brodin Mitchell glares at her. Cathode continues the cheesy grin as she passes him and hugs her aunt. Ms. Nelson hugs her back and smiles past her at Brodin.

"I'll take her from here. Thank you Mr. Mitchell."

"You're welcome, Miss Nelson."

Cathode and Ms. Nelson turn and enter the facility proper from the front security room. Head of Security Brodin Mitchell watches them, most specifically Ms. Nelson, leave until the door whooshes shut. He spins his chair back around and eyes the contents of his "Unsecured Electronics" bin. Cathode's bracelet is stuck to the side of the metal bowl. He tries, unsuccessfully, to remove it. Or, for that matter, the bowl itself from his metal desk. A small blue LED blinks inside one of the jewels on the band indicating the industrial grade electromagnet band is still powered. Head of Security Brodin Mitchell breathes out heavily through his nose before turning back to his security screens.

Cathode holds her arm around her aunt's waist as they walk down the corridor.

"So, A-Bridge... are you ever going to ask McGruff the security dog out on a date?"

Putting her arm on her niece's shoulder Ms. Nelson looks off into the distance. She pinches Cathode's shoulder.

"I don't think so. And I know you like your nicknames, Catherine, but I'm not so fond of A-Bridge. Aunt Bridget, Auntie, Bridget, Auntie Nelson. Those all work. A-Bridge makes me sound like a piece of computer hardware."

"What's wrong with that? And you've got to call me Cathode or I won't feel cool and you'll ruin my self esteem and I'll get expelled from school and all that horribleness will be on your head, madam."

"I'll cut you a deal. You call me what I want to be called and I'll call you what you want to be called... at least when your mother's not around."

"Deal, Auntie B."

Bridget shoots Cathode a frustrated side glance.

"Auntie Bridget."

"Perfect, Cathode."

"So, is he just like a total creeper or something?"

"Who? Brodin? I mean, Mister Mitchell? No, it's just... Co-workers and time. And things like that. I guess, maybe it's a bit complicated for a high school student to comprehend."

"Hey, I've a job. I've got, uh, co-workers. I'm smart."

"Right. Not what I meant."

"Uh-huh. Sure."

Bridget smiles at Cathode and squeezes her shoulder again. They walk through a second set of doors. As they walk down the corridor off to the right Cathode looks through a large window into a science lab. In the middle of the lab surrounded by a grid of lasers, scopes, computers and other devices a cantaloupe hovers above the ground suspended within a strange metal contraption. Cathode's eyes widen as they continue to walk past.

"What's with the cantaloupe?!"

"Oh. I'll tell you later."

"Huh."

They round the corner headed off to the left and toward a set of double doors. Bridget pulls her security badge from her retractable lanyard and presses it to a pad next to the door frame. There is a buzz and the heavy click of a serious mechanical lock disengaging. Bridget releases her badge, which whips back to place at her hip, and pushes the heavy doors open.

"If you want to see some really cool science I'll show what we've finally got built. Check this out!"

Cathode freezes in her tracks. She practically trips over herself stepping forward. Bridget holds her arms out wide as they enter a massive warehouse sized lab. She spins around with a large smile on her face but Cathode doesn't see it. Her gaze is fixed upon the large matte black shuttlecraft currently parked in the center of the lab. It's supported by a odd assortment of metal trestle. The ship itself doesn't touch the floor due to a set of massive hexagonally rings, mounted near the rear of the ship, that circle the width of the ship. Bridget remains smiling as Cathode's jaw goes slack.

"Pretty cool, yeah?"

Cathode has to shake her head a little bit.

"What is... what is that?"

"It's Superfluous."

"Sue per flow us? Is that Latin?"

Bridget puts her hand on Cathode's back and ushers her closer to the ship.

"We nicknamed it the Superfluous. It's got a long ridiculously intricate serial number officially. But, we hated trying to rattle that off. So, we just gave it that nickname as a sort of joke. It stuck. Thought you'd be just the right type of person to appreciate that."

Cathode steps up next to the ship. She leans in toward the rings system, afraid to touch the immaculate shiny dark gray surface. She notices the first ring is just small enough to squeeze through the second larger ring if needed. The ship itself is like a sleek futuristic RV mixed with a floating tank.

"This thing is so thermal!"

"You don't even know the half of it. What you're looking at there is the Spatial Brim."

"It's a hat for your ship?"

Bridget lets out a quick laugh. Other scientists working in the area peek from their stations to see what is going on. Once they see it's Bridget talking to her niece they go right back to work. Bridget walks around to the front of the ship.

"In a way I suppose it is. The ship can't really go out and do its job without the quantum rings."

"The quantum rings?"

"Yes, well, this gets a bit complicated but the system we've built into the Superfluous is based on quantum theory and zero point energy."

"... Say what?"

"Oh boy. Well, the basic point is the engine system can gain energy basically exponentially from a very minute source."

"Like a battery? Or some sort of fuel cell?"

"Not even that much. It can start its exponential looping growth from something as simple as normal background radiation."

"Wow. So, like you could super charge it by parking it near a star?"

"Technically, yes. Good observation. But, that would be an immense amount of starting energy. Absolutely more than necessary. Possibly, dangerously so. I might have to make a note to get that actual equation. You see the engine takes its energy and feeds it into this ring system. The larger ring here can be detached from the unit and still be building from the same receiving charge. Once they reach a full charge the smaller ring will shift forward to in front of the ship and open an ingress, of sorts. The exit of that portal opens on the larger ring and the ship travels through it reconnecting both rings after it exits the larger one."

Cathode stands rigid with her eyes wide, locked on her aunt.

"Did you just... Did- Did you just describe instantaneously teleporting a spaceship?"

Bridget beams wide again. She hugs her niece lightly with one arm while continuing to walk around the rest of the ship with her.

"See, I knew you'd get it. Now, not completely instantaneously. Obviously. But, very close to it, yes. It still physically travels forward."

"Wait, you're serious? This thing opens up, like, a wormhole and you just pop through it to wherever you left the big ring?"

"Yes. In theory. But, it's just an untested prototype at this point presently."

Cathode stops as Bridget continues her slow guided tour walk around the ship. Cathode put her hands to her eyes as if she'd been asleep. She can't believe what she's hearing.

"This. This thing. This is incredible."

"Want to sit in it?"

Cathode's knees almost give out on her.

"Seriously?! YES! A billion trillion times yes!"

Cathode takes a few leaping steps toward Bridget who has walked over to a nearby wheel cart filled with pieces of equipment. Bridget picks up a small black rectangular box the size of a pack of chewing gum and a heavy duty work tablet. Carrying both she returns to the back of the Superfluous. Bridget clicks a button on the little rectangle. A heavy mechanical lock clicks and the back end of the ship splits horizontally in the center, opening into its cargo hold like a ramp. Bridget hops in as the bottom door clicks to a stop a few inches from the lab floor. She turns around and helps Cathode up into the cargo hold. Bridget clicks another button on the cube and the split rear doors begin to close.

"What is that thing?"

Bridget holds up the little black box and then drops it into Cathode's hand.

"It's a key fob. An antique piece of security for mostly earth bound vehicles. Not sure when we decided to use one but it just seemed to fit with the absurdity of the project."

"So, you need this to unlock the ship?"

"Yes. Well, not really. You can still just unlock it manually, from the inside. Or with one of our RFID-ed suits when they're finally built. But, you can't really get in without one of those otherwise. There are no other doors besides the back currently. No window to stick a clothes hanger in, you know."

Bridget notices Cathode has no idea what that joke actually means and continues.

"That's the real reason for it. Made sense as a security step we were required to put in, in some manner."

"Required?"

"Yeah, don't worry about that. This thing won't be flying anytime soon."

Cathode steps into the cockpit area and plops down in the co-pilot chair. She spins it around toward Bridget.

"Well, the only real question left is; when do I start my internship already?"

Bridget smiles at her niece and sits down gently in the pilot chair. She hands the work tablet she's been carrying to Cathode. Cathode's eyes widen. The paperwork on the tablet display is for an internship at Navitus Immensus Labs. Cathode's eyes pinch shut as she's almost about to cry.

"Your mom is going to need to sign it too since it involves a pretty strict NDA agreement. But, we're all set on the lab side. I'm not sure what you're making at the grocery store but this will probably be significantly more. As it does come with a lot more responsibilities."

Cathode fights back tears of joy. She leaps from the co-pilot chair and hugs Bridget tight.

"Ok... OK! You get your mom to sign and bring the tablet back on your first day. The agreement is hardlocked to the device for biometric security reasons. I was thinking, maybe, next week for your first day?"

Still holding on firmly Cathode nods her head into Bridget's shoulder. Finally loosening her grip Cathode sits back down in the co-pilot chair. She hides her giant smile behind the tablet as she looks enduringly at her aunt through tear filled eyes. Bridget notices the damp spots Cathode's eyes left on her shoulder.

"I think it might be time for you to go though. You've got another job to finish before you can start here."

Cathode's face drops.

"Oh no! I'm supposed to give my two weeks right? Like, I can't just drop the grocery gig. Right?"

"I'm sure your manager will be fine if you find a suitable replacement before coming here. Have any friends looking for work?"

Bridget gets up and starts to head back into the ship's cargo hold. Cathode thinks for a moment before following after her. Bridget clicks the key fob, unlocking the back doors.

"Lazy!"

"What?"

"Not a what. Who. My friend La- Bradley. I'm pretty sure his dad has been hounding him to get a job. I guarantee he'd do it for me."

As they exit the back of Superfluous Bridget clicks the key fob one last time, causing the doors to slowly, automatically close.

"That sounds perfect. And your boyfriend-"

"Hey! Friend. Not, boyfriend."

"Sorry, sorry! Your friend, who is a boy, I would believe he should suffice."

"Good."

"Great!"

Cathode looks back toward the entrance corridor. They begin to walk back toward the entrance.

"So, what's with the cantaloupe?"

"Oh, right. Yeah, nothing."

"What? But it looks like some wild experiment. Antigravity or something."

"Nope. It's a piece of postmodern art gifted to the lab. Just a metal sculpture with a fancy looking quantum levitation plate in the middle."

"And the cantaloupe?"

"Just an everyday ordinary melon. Like the ones you've delivered to us. I'm fairly sure you delivered us the current one actually. Someone initially put a bunch of bananas in there as a joke. Now, we use it as a way to see if people coming in are paying attention to what's going on. And to chill snacks. Does that pretty well."

As they pass the large lab window again Cathode realizes the sculpture is sitting on a low black display stand in the middle of the lab. Far from any of the actual equipment.

"So, people notice it a lot?"

"Surprisingly not. You're one of, maybe, a half dozen to mention it. Good eyes. Runs in the family."

Bridget winks at Cathode.

"Now, give your auntie a hug and get home."

Cathode hugs Bridget one last time and leaves the lab.

Cathode parks the grocery truck into its stall. As she's hopping out she has her goggles on and is talking to Lazy.

"It's super binary simple. You can even set the delivery truck to autopilot and watch videos if you really want to... Just don't tell Jeremy I said that. Right. Yeah, I'm back at the store now. I'll totally set you up."

Knocking and entering all at once Cathode steps into Jeremy's office, catching him mid-slurp on a cup of instant noodles. He slowly slurps up the noodles he has caught with his chopsticks.

"Who could be knocking at my door? Yes, please. Now, you may enter..."

"Hilarious! I'm going to sit now."

A bit awkwardly Cathode slides into the seat in front of Jeremy's desk.

"I'm not going to like this talk, am I?" Jeremy questions as he slides his half eaten dinner to the side.

"Maybe. I think you might. I quit."

Jeremy is legitimately shocked. Cathode freezes in a "now hold on" pose.

"But! But, I am going to get you a top notch replacement and train them before I bid adios to this popsicle stand."

"I understood the first part but almost none of that last bit."

"You need to watch Mork & Mindy. It's really funny."

"I'm not entirely sure I know what that is either. Wait! Quitting for what now? Keep this on the proper topic."

"My aunt set me up with an internship at her lab. I've got to take that opportunity, Jeremy. And I can't work both jobs."

"Well, that is understandable."

"Right? You'd never be able to get rid of me otherwise. I'd be here. For. Ever."

"I want to laugh but I feel like that's true. I'd also like to get back to my noodles. Bring in your replacement next shift and I'll set up an evaluation."

"Thank you so much Jeremy! Perfect. Awesome. Cool. Cool. Great. Thermal."

Cathode sits beaming. Jeremy stares at her for a moment and side eyes his dinner.

"Oh! Right. Yeah, get back to that bountiful feast there."

"No need to be rude."

Spinning out of her chair Cathode heads to the door. She turns her head with a look of real caring.

"I'm just saying. You work in a grocery store. You could be eating almost any amazing thing."

Jeremy blinks a few times, looks down at the cup of noodles on his desk and slowly stirs the contents.

"I could. But... This grounds me. It reminds me of a time when I didn't have anything and even a small cup like this was a treasure. Sometimes in life you need a reminder of how little you need to be happy and be grateful for all that you have."

Cathode leans against the door frame between Jeremy's office and the grocery store. Her eyes water slightly and her lips curl into an awkward little smile.

"When I do finally leave, please, write that in a card for me. That's really a beautiful thought, Jeremy."

"Thank you, Catherine."

She waves as she leaves, letting the office door swing shut. Jeremy sits in silence for a moment. Looking at a digital picture frame on his desk he sniffs lightly and then picks up his cup of noodles.

Strutting out the front of the grocery store Cathode slides her goggles on, irises open, and sends a connect request to Lazy. He picks up immediately.

Because of course you do.

"Yeah, so?"

"Polite. Good news and bad news."

"Wait, how is there bad news? What happened?"

"Good news-"

"But! But! The bad!?"

"Ahem! The good news is this; Jeremy is willing to give you an evaluation. So, I mean, I vouched for you so the job is basically already yours."

"Awesome!"

Cathode stops at a street light waiting for the walk signal. She gets distracted for a moment as a man in light green robes, kneeling on a small mat, begins chanting kitty-corner from her. He seems to be staring directly at her as he chants, nodding his head with the rhythm only he seems to know. When he bends at the waist in rhythm with his chanting Cathode sees his sunburst haircut and dim LED crystal. The walk signal flashes on and Cathode snaps out of her semi-trance.

"Hello? Bad news?!"

"Oh, right. So, I think it's amazing news but I mean you might not since you'll be my driver. My valet. My taxi man. My taxi driver. Well, maybe not that last one. Not like that movie."

"Huh? I got two jobs?"

"Well, one pays and the other just happens to be a benefit of working at a place on my- I'm sorry. Your new delivery route."

"Oh, I get it. That is acceptable bad news. It's bad. But not, like, grotesque."

"You want grotesque?"

"Nope! Hell no."

With that Lazy disconnects and Cathode chuckles into her hands a little at his reaction and the potential of her new job. She taps her goggles and loads up a movie screen to look like it's floating far enough ahead of her that she can still watch where she's walking. She pauses for a moment to be sure her goggles hear her command.

"Apply collision immediacy patch version two point seven."

A grid of white light suddenly appears over the edges of everything in Cathode's view. It flickers, disappears and then slowly reloads itself. For a test Cathode walks directly toward a street sign post. The post goes from having a muted, nearly invisible green grid around it to a flashing solid red grid. Cathode sighs slightly, steps around the post and unpauses her movie.

See that brain? Red means dead. Let's try to remember that.

Taking one last glance over her shoulder she makes eye contact again with the chanting man. He continues to chant and nod but doesn't break his stare. His lips begin to curl into a strange smile. Cathode speeds up her walk a bit to get around the corner of the next building.

Although she's relaxed, being away from the chanting grinning man, Cathode picks up her speed even more to slow jog. She darts between pedestrians, her goggles relaying red grids over the people and other sidewalk hazards. A smirk grows across Cathode's lips as the program keeps up when she sometimes intentionally runs directly at objects.

Reaching the corner to her apartment building she breaks into a full sprint. Charging directly at the playground equipment in the park in front of the building she leaps over a spring rider in the shape of a duck. Cathode slides on the rubber mulch between the A frame of the swing set. She reaches the swing set's slide and plants a hand on it to side vault over it. Her smile immediately disappears as her hand loses its grip on the slide surface and she lands hard on her shoulder. Her momentum pushes her forward and she flips over, face planting in the rubber mulch. Slowly, she sits up and brushes off her goggles' lenses. Spitting out a bit of mulch she peels the goggles off her face.

Noted. Still not a parkour athlete.

Standing up Cathode brushes her pants off and spits rubber again. She fits her goggles back over her eyes and taps them to life. Walking with a slight limp she heads into the apartment building.

"Note; possibly add trajectory clairvoyance program version three to collision immediacy in the new patch. End note."

Entering her apartment she is still talking to her goggles.

"Load current build of trajectory clairvoyance to Gizmoto now."

From the hallway Cathode can hear Gizmoto booting up inside her bedroom. As she enters her room Gizmoto is on her desk. His eyes are fluttering as the new program is uploading to his memory. When the install completes Gizmoto leaps to his feet and stands at attention. Cathode takes off her goggles, turns them over, and gently taps them over her trash can to dislodge any more rubber mulch. She walks over to her desk and grabs a can of compressed air to clean them more thoroughly. Gizmoto starts to pick at his belly button as one of his idle animations kicks on. The motion catches Cathode's attention. She looks from Gizmoto on her desk to her bed.

"Gizmoto, load trajectory clairvoyance and link with my goggles."

Gizmoto flicks his fingers like he has belly button lint on them before standing at the ready. Cathode points in the air at Gizmoto and then points to her bed. She slides her desk chair between them somewhat bridging the gap.

"Gizmoto, go."

The little robot bear takes two steps back as, in Cathode's goggles, an orange dotted line makes two curved arches from the desk, to the chair, to the bed. Gizmoto takes off running, just before it reaches the edge of the desk it leaps, landing perfectly on the chair's armrest and then leaps again right onto the bed. He lands into a forward roll and stands up facing Cathode. She throws her hands up in the air.

"Touchdown!"

Gizmoto throws his hands up in the air mimicking her.

"Success dance!"

Gizmoto begins doing a silly robot dance on the bed as Cathode triggers her room speakers to play an upbeat song. She spins around and falls backward onto the bed. She grabs the still dancing Gizmoto and snuggles with him for a moment. She winces.

"Gizmoto, remind me to program you to give massages."

Still wrapped in her arms, Gizmoto gives an affirmative nod.

Cathode hears the front door open.

"Catherine? Are you home?"

Cathode's mother, Constance, calls out from the front door.

"I need a hand."

With a soft sigh, Cathode rolls off of her bed and plods out to the hallway. As soon as she turns her head the tiredness of the day drains away. She sees that her mother is carrying grocery bags.

"Huoguo?! We're doing huoguo tonight?"

Cathode rushes over to help grab several of the small bags her mother is juggling in the doorway. Cathode opens one on the way back to the kitchen.

"And we got synth-b? What's the special occasion?"

Slipping out of her shoes and into her slippers, Constance sets her work satchel down and unbuttons her jacket as she follows her daughter into the kitchen.

"Dad sent a video with the note to get this for dinner tonight. So..."

"So, probably good news."

"Probably good news. Yes."

Placing their bags on the counter next to the sink the two begin sorting the contents. Constance holds up two soup base bags so Cathode can read the labels.

"What do you think? Tomato or curry tonight?"

"Curry! Until the heat death of the universe. Curry. Should I chop mushrooms?"

"Yes, thank you. There should be a box of them in the bags. The ones in the fridge went bad a few days ago."

Cathode pulls out the mushroom box, grabs the curry soup base bag from her mother and walks over to the kitchen table. Before she puts her items down she taps a control panel on the wall behind the table. The screen flickers to life and Cathode taps the "CONFIG 3" option when it appears. She waits a moment as the kitchen table splits out from its center like pie slices. The wedges of table top roll out far enough to reveal a metal pot built into the central cylinder base of the table. The pot rises and locks into place. The points of the table top wedges flip down a few inches from the center to leave space for the pot. Then the wedges slide back into the center under the cooking pot. Cathode nods while sticking out her lower jaw.

Not a bad addition, dad. Not bad at all. Very useful.

Cathode dumps the curry soup base out of the bag and into the cooking pot. Constance brings over a filtered water pitcher and pours it into the pot until the soup reaches the fill line. Cathode spins a chair up to the table. She grabs a knife from the magnetized knife rack on the wall and a plastic cutting board out of a drawer. As she pulls the stems off and cuts the mushrooms into large chunks her mother pours an assortment of frozen fish balls into a bowl. Cathode scoops up the mushroom chunks and using her elbow she taps on the sink to clean them. Constance pulls down a second large bowl for her. Cathode dumps the mushrooms into the bowl and grabs two heads of purple romaine lettuce from the fridge.

Cathode begins to peel leaves off the lettuce when she hears the front door slide open. Her brother grunts as he tosses something heavy up onto the landing past the entrance. The sound of wooden rods rattling together stirs Cathode's memory.

Kendo. That's it. He joined the kendo team. I totally knew that.

Cathode, grinning like she just solved a coding problem, peels another leaf off the head of lettuce and tosses it into the large bowl next to the sink. Constance lets out an audible gasp.

"Mikko, what happened to your head?!"

Mikko sniffs and grunts again. Cathode puts down the half peeled head and peeks around the kitchen wall at her brother and mother. Her mom is holding back Mikko's hair revealing a two inch long fairly shallow cut. The skin around it is slightly bruised with three butterfly bandages holding the cut shut. Mikko slides on his house slippers and brushes his mom's hand away.

"It's nothing, ma. Cool down. Yasu was blaming his helmet for not being able to get a strike. So, I told him, take it off and let's see."

Constance stands with her arms crossed, obviously upset, as Mikko grabs his bogu bag and begins to drag it toward his room.

"Mikko!"

Cathode lets out a solitary "ha" and nods, chin out, in approval at her brother from the kitchen. He smirks at her and wipes his nose, sniffing again.

I probably shouldn't have told him 'tough guys' do that sniffing thing. Eh, it's pretty funny though.

"Cath gets it, ma. Besides you should see Yasu. He's got a bruise mohawk now. Totally has to grow his hair out again. Probably, like, made it permanently part down the middle now. Pow!"

Mikko makes a chopping motion with his free hand. Constance is no less upset at her son.

"Mikko, stop."

"It's fine. He's fine. I'm fine. He said he's going to train harder with his helmet on. Also, Sensei Tanaka already disciplined us."

Mikko reaches his bedroom door and, with the quick twist at his waist, whips the bag of kendo gear into the room. It clatters somewhere in the dark, sounding like most of its contents spilled out. Constance lets out another sigh and shakes her head. She walks to the fridge as she talks.

"Well, that's good, I guess. Just clean up for dinner."

Mikko looks to the converted kitchen table.

"Oh zap. We're doing hotpot?"

Cathode uses the sink hose faucet attachment to spritz clean the lettuce leaves in the bowl and walks it to the table.

"Believe it."

"Curry?"

"Curry."

"I'll be right back!"

Almost tripping in his loose slippers Mikko sprints to their shared bathroom. Constance places two containers of synthetic meat on the table. One beef and one pork. Cathode lets out a low whistle.

"Dad must have good news if we're getting two types of synth."

Constance sits down, somewhat heavily, and peels off the safety seal edge of synthetic meat packages.

"It'll just be nice to see his face."

Cathode realizes her mother's face looks tired. She reaches out and pats the top of her mom's left hand. Constance sets down the torn safety seals and places her right hand on top of Cathode's.

"Yeah, mom. It will."

A toilet flushes and a door opens with the reverberating metal twang of bouncing off a coiled door stop. Constance pats her daughter's hands and stands up turning her head to the hallway.

"Wash your hands!"

Mikko, having just reached the entrance door of his bedroom, freezes.

"Sorry. Sorry. Sorry."

He spins around and runs back to the bathroom. Constance throws the torn safety seals into the composter. She takes down three small white porcelain bowls, closes the cabinet with her shoulder and opens a drawer with her free hand. Cathode hops up and grabs the bowls from her.

"Xie xie."

"Mei shi, mama."

Constance pulls out three sets of metal chopsticks, white plastic soup spoons and a metal wire mesh scoop. They set the table as Mikko skids into the kitchen. He tears a stack of napkins out of a holder and plops into his chair. The automated table hot pot has already reached optimal temperature. Cathode drops in a few of her mushroom chunks and lettuce. Constance adds several of the frozen fish balls. Mikko reaches for the meat but Constance uses her chopsticks to block his.

"Wait. Dad sent a video. We should watch it before we start eating."

Mikko rubs his upper gums with his chopsticks.

"Hope it's short."

Cathode shoots Mikko a look of "don't". He pulls the chopsticks out of his mouth and sits up straight.

"I mean. I hope it's good. News. The video is good news."

Constance squints her eyes at her son for a moment before tapping her watch. The wall in the living room straight across from the kitchen table shimmers and powers on. A blurry pink image appears frozen on the video wall. Tapping her watch again Cathode's mom starts the video message. On the video wall a camera view shakes and moves up and away from Cathode's dad's hand revealing the blurred image was his palm. The tiny camera drone he shot the video with backs away from him until his upper body to top of his head is visible and in focus. It wiggles ever so slightly as it holds position. He looks at his own watch which is a matching twin of Cathode's mom's.

"Recording? Good. Ok. Yes? Wait..."

He checks the watch again.

"Nope. Right the first time. Recording. I should probably edit these things or fix that record light. Or... Uh, hello family. Catherine. Mikko. Constance."

Mikko stifles a laugh.

"He remembered our names."

Constance shushes him as Cathode's dad, Biao, continues talking.

"Hope everyone is doing well. Staying out of trouble. Both of you. Out of trouble. Emphasis here. And you're helping out your mother. Equally as important. Um, yeah. Anyway, it's been busy out here which is why there hasn't been a comm in a while. When was the last one. Uh, hmm. Wait."

Biao pauses and stares off into the distance. He adjusts the industrial style goggles he's always wearing. Cathode feels they are almost certainly fused to his skin at this point as she remembers seeing him sleeping with them still on when he was working at the lunar Phalanx North Mining Outpost. Biao snaps out of his trance.

"Three months. Feels like three here. Anyway, it's been busy, as I said. There have been some big expansions out here and, long story short, I'm now one of the lead Cultural Resource Management Archeologists for the Ares Prospecting

Division. So, yeah. Woohoo and all that. I trust mom picked up a nice celebratory feast for you."

Biao's smile fades and he looks down at the ground for a moment. Cathode lets out a low exhale.

"Here it comes. Again."

Constance shuts her eyes tightly for a moment. Biao looks up into his drone camera.

"That also, obviously, means I won't be back next month. Changing positions and divisions has required me to move a lot of things and I won't make the crew charter flight back."

Yup. Again.

"But. But, I will definitely be back for Lunar New Year. The promotion comes with an extra two weeks of required paid time off. So, just a little bit longer but I shall, uh, return. Eat a couple of those filled fish balls I like. Yeah, ok. Love you guys."

Biao taps his phone and waves into the camera as the drone powers down and flies into his waving hand. The video finishes and the file closes automatically. The video wall flickers off and returns to a blank wall. Constance opens her eyes and smiles.

"Required. They pulled his file. Well, that's better than I thought."

Mikko has lifted several strips of raw synth-beef and is holding them over the boiling pot. Constance nods at him. Cathode notices her mom blinking a few times to clear her eyes.

"He'll make the flight this time, mom. I mean, it is required. They might chain him to a seat but he'll come back."

Constance puts her hand on Cathode's shoulder and squeezes softly. Mikko dumps several frozen fish balls into the pot and stirs it. He quickly pulls, blows on and then chews a piece of cooked synth-beef. Cathode swirls the broth and pulls out her own piece. Constance pulls out a piece of wilted lettuce and a mushroom chunk. She looks at both of her children trying not to burn their mouths as they eat.

"Taste good?"

"Great!"

"Haochi!"

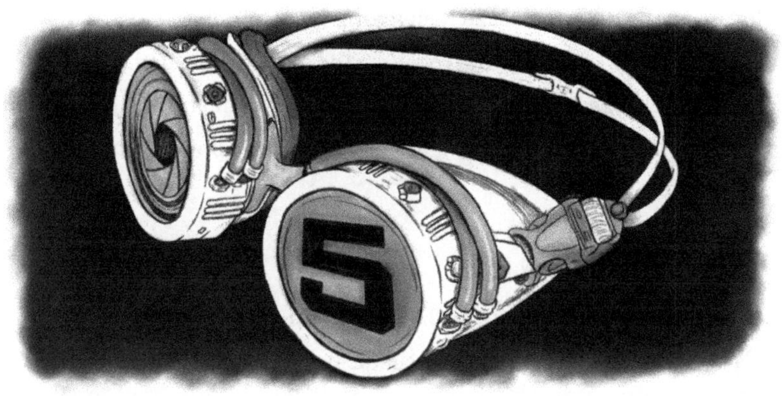

"I just want to warn you that your new boss is a crazy person. He is going to yell at you and it's just normal. That's how it is. That's what he does. Don't worry about it. Just stand tall and don't let him get too pushy."

Cathode stands outside Jeremy's office giving a pep talk to Lazy.

"You are aware I've met Jeremy? Numerous times in fact."

"Yes. But, at work he's like a caged mongoose."

"I wouldn't make that comparison. I don't see Jeremy slaying cobras. Maybe more of a koala. Like a drop bear."

The door to Jeremy's office swings open.

"And you two are aware this door is super flimsy? I could hear you just fine."

Lazy looks a bit mortified but Cathode just smiles.

"I knew."

"I- I am now, sir. I'm Bradley, sir. Brad for short. Might I say thank you for this opportunity I won't-"

"Relax Bradley. This isn't the military. And if Catherine can do this job I think even a mongoose could do it."

"Hey!"

"What? Mongooses can beat cobras."

"Wait. Really?"

Jeremy smirks at Cathode and then returns his attention to Lazy.

"The only deliveries going out today are the mining office and... technically that's it but I've agreed to let you taxi Catherine to her internship. Just do that last so she can show you everything you need to do for delivery at the mine."

"Yes, sir."

"Stop that. Just call me Jeremy."

"Yes, sir... Jeremy. Uh..."

"I'm also not a knight. Now, go. Before I do turn into a drop bear."

Cathode takes her time explaining all the basic steps of loading and driving the delivery truck up and out of the city.

As they're leaving the city's vehicular airlock Lazy taps his helmet a few times. He shakes his head.

"Ah crap!"

"What? What is it?

With one hand Lazy scrapes at his helmet, trying to remove it. He catches the latch with his thumb and digs his fingers under it. As he tries to flip off his helmet he cranks the steering wheel to the side.

"Whoa! Don't do that!"

Cathode leans across and pushes the wheel back. She taps on the autopilot controls and the delivery truck turns, straightening its path up the exit lane path. Lazy peels his goggles off his face in a panic. He drops them to his lap and grabs the steering wheel tight with both hands.

"Sorry! Sorry! Full popcorn!"

Lazy relaxes his grip as he realizes the delivery truck is on autopilot. He blinks a few times and rubs his eyes. Cathode looks to the goggles in Lazy's lap. Both the lenses are flashing a blinding white light.

"What did you do?"

Looking sheepishly, Lazy picks up his goggles and hands them over to Cathode.

"Might have sideloaded a few old unstable terran OSes for some deep diving in an absolutely ancient Arc. Might have."

Cathode holds down the power on Lazy's goggles causing them to go into a full power cycle. She pulls a cable from a spool on the band of her own goggles, hidden behind her ear. She plugs the connector ending into Lazy's goggles before the base OS has rebooted. She flicks her fingers in the air to load up some of her diagnostic tools.

"And that caused a full kernel panic?"

"I might have forgotten to shut down all of them, which I had running all at once, before I came into work today. Might have. Might be that. Think you can fix that?"

"You think?"

Cathode runs a storage scan on Lazy's goggles and laughs.

"You also have, like, no space on here. I'm going to have to delete something to make some space to repair those OSes. If you still need them."

Lazy considers his options for a moment.

"Yeah, I'd like to keep those for the time being. I'm looking for some very specific stuff. You can toss media folders one through four. I already clouded those for sure."

The cab of the truck begins to rumble and Lazy looks up in terror. A mining truck pulls past them.

"Aya!"

Cathode deletes the four media folders and sets her repair tool to focus on the different operating system partitions in Lazy's storage. The tool begins running. Cathode opens her goggles' irises to look at the passing truck.

"You get used to them. That's not even a big one."

"It's not? Jees, I really need to get out more. Or not. I suppose this is big enough for me. Indoors are safe."

"The big boys will be out when we get closer to the offices."

"Oh. Oh, boy. The big boys. Yes, lucky us."

Cathode's scan completes with a faint chime. She closes her irises again to finish the fix.

"Resetting the BIOS on two of these. I'm also going to give you a virtual machine app I've got that will contain all of them. Keeps things cleaner. Less likely any of them will go full popcorn."

Lazy is still staring at the massive truck getting further away from them.

"All of those words sound like good things. Go for it."

In Cathode's goggles she installs her virtual machine app and moves a few more files around in Lazy's storage. She sets his goggles to full reset.

"Should be good to go after this reboot."

Lazy's goggles give off a light electronic whir. The different irises open and close. Cathode quickly cycles through each of the OSes making sure they all run clean. Satisfied with her work, Cathode opens her irises and goes to remove the repair cable from Lazy's goggles. Before she can, a chat alert pops up on Lazy's screen. An alert from Margaret. Cathode pulls out the repair cable and gives it a small tug, causing it to auto recoil behind her ear.

"You've got a message from Manticore."

"Oh? Did you work your magic already? Am I cleared to hunt for more treasures of the unknown?"

Cathode flicks her wrist, tossing Lazy his goggles.

"All good. Just remember to share the good stuff."

"Thanks. Will do."

Lazy slides his goggles back on and opens the message from Margaret. He chuckles and selects a file to send back to her. Cathode purses her lips to the side of her face. She looks straight ahead.

"What did she want?"

"Huh? Oh. Well, remember that movie I sent you that had the zombie baby scene?"

"Might have to narrow that down. There were a few. But, I think I know which you mean. Rat mommy?"

"Ha! Yeah. That one. We were just talking about something related and I thought I'd already sent that to you both. She said she never saw it, so just giving it to her now. Good stuff."

"She's going to enjoy that one. And by enjoy, I mean hate your guts for not warning her about the custard scene."

"True. And we know this because I didn't warn you either. But, who wants something that amazing spoiled for them? Really?"

"Me. I did. It's super gross. If I had been eating I would have barfed."

"So, what I'm hearing is; tell her to be eating while watching?"

Cathode stifles a laugh and playfully punches Lazy in the arm.

"No. You butt."

Lazy smirks and slides his helmet back over his now working goggles. He locks the latch and shakes his head back and forth to make sure it's stuck on.

"Alright, we're close to the mining office. I think I'll take control again."

Just as Lazy grips onto the steering wheel one of the real big mining trucks turns onto the road coming toward them. Lazy slides his hands off the wheel.

"Maybe later."

Cathode nods in agreement, looking out the front windshield. She notices a small envelope wedged into the frame behind the dash display in front of her. She pulls it out. The envelope has "Catherine" written on the front. Lazy looks over at it.

"What's that?"

"I don't know."

Cathode unlocks one of her gloves so she can open the envelope. Using her nail to slice open the envelope she peers inside it and smiles. With her ungloved hand she pulls out a greeting card in the shape of an opened cup of noodles. She opens the card. Inside there is a handwritten note; "Catherine, I know you're going to go far. Just remember the little things. Best of luck in the future! - Jeremy". Lazy glances over at Cathode as she gingerly places the card into her satchel bag. He notices her eyes have watered slightly as she locks her glove back in place.

Filled with mochi from Mrs. Takigasaki and having successfully done his first delivery Lazy pulls the delivery vehicle up to the front entrance of Navitas Immensus Laboratories. He enters with Cathode who almost sprints ahead of him in excitement. McGruffyduffydo greets them as they enter with his normal blunt, uninterested face. Cathode slides up to his desk and slaps the top of it.

"I can tell you're as excited as I am for my first day of work! I don't think I've ever seen you smile so much."

Mr. Mitchell stares straight ahead. Not even a twitch.

"Alright! This is my chauffeur-"

"Hey!"

Lazy, who had been looking in awe at the facility, snaps to glare at Cathode.

"Driver?"

"Yeah, that's fine."

"My driver here is also taking over my old delivery route so he'll need to be properly vetted, deloused and what not so he can bring you all those sodas you like so much."

A small smile creeps across Mr. Mitchell's lips.

"I do like my sodas. Your aunt is waiting for you. Here's your limited, and I mean LIMITED, access card. Do not lose it."

In quick motion Cathode snatches the card from Mr. Mitchell's hand, sprints to the security door access pad and shouts back at Lazy.

"All set! My aunt is going to give me a ride home tonight. Thank you chauffeur!"

"Hey!"

The security door beeps and slides open. Cathode turns around after she's entered and waves back at Lazy.

"Kidding!"

Lazy rocks on his heels a bit.

"Right."

The security door shuts and Lazy continues to look around the facilities' security area until he hears a tapping. Mr. Mitchell is holding out a tablet and pen with delivery security clearance paperwork on it.

"Ah. Right."

Lazy begins to fill it out. HE raises his eyes sheepishly.

"I promise I won't be as annoying as she is, sir."

Mr. Mitchell grins.

"Good to know."

Picking up a pair of safety goggles and heavy rubber gloves from an equipment shelf Cathode struts over to her Aunt.

"I'm ready. Where's the fission reactor at?"

Cathode snaps the rubber glove on her hand.

"Cute. Put them back. You've got real work to do."

"Thermal!"

Quickly, but with care to place the equipment exactly where she took them, Cathode puts the gloves and safety glasses back. She stands at attention in front of Bridget. Bridget smiles and leads her to a computer terminal.

"So, my first task is programming something?"

"Not really, I'm afraid. Your first official task will be the super exciting vital, life saving, massively important file archiving!"

Cathode's posture droops as she sits in the chair. Bridget puts a hand on her shoulder.

"We need you to organize and run encryption on our outdated files before they're beamed to a failsafe backup off site. It is actually important work."

Readjusting to sit straight up Cathode cracks her knuckles over the keyboard surface.

"Understood. Is it okay if I use my goggles while I work?"

"You can't run any wireless system. Wouldn't really matter if you tried due to the faraday cage shielding of this building. But, it'd get you in trouble if detected. And you can't run the goggles video or camera functions."

"So... I can wear them for the headphones to play some music?"

"As long as it's music stored locally, absolutely. Just nothing too loud that the rest of the lab can hear it, obviously."

"Obviously."

Bridget taps on the screen causing it to wake up from sleep mode. A small note document is open on the screen.

"This note is your basic work load list. It doesn't have an end date so don't feel like you've got to rush anything. Once you get to step five you can run the verifier to double check all files required for export are properly encrypted, compressed and filed. I already logged you into this terminal. You can change your login if you want. The current password is your mom's birthday. I trust you know what that is?"

Cathode sits, staring blankly at the screen for a moment.

"I think I'll change my password."

"Cathode."

"Joke. But, I seriously always change from a premade with whatever I'm working on."

"Absolutely fine. You know where the break room and bathrooms are. So, if there aren't any other questions I'll leave you to it for a few hours and check back to see how it's going."

"Roger, Auntie Bridget."

Bridget pats Cathode's shoulder and leaves her to work. Cathode slips her goggles out of her satchel bag, straps them on, selects a premade playlist of music, slides the visor up and begins opening folders on the terminal in front of her. She peeks back at Bridget who is working on a terminal near the Superfluous. She smiles and then quickly returns to her filing work.

Sitting at her terminal, now slightly cluttered with office supplies and her own random tchotchkes, Cathode sips from a can of soda.

McGruff won't miss just one. I'll remember to have Lazy add an extra case to the normal order. This sour apple is pretty good.

She sets the can down in a magnetized thermos coaster. Cathode taps enter on her terminal keyboard and a compiler program pops up on screen with a percentage bar. The bar slowly fills. Cathode leans back and stretches, arms raised to the ceiling, spinning in her chair as she does. As the chair slowly rotates Cathode notices Bridget speaking to a high ranking member of the Lunar Frontiersmen off near a restricted area. She's not sure of his position but from all the medals on the older man's uniform it must be fairly high up. He is flanked by two lower level marines. Bridget is describing something related to the key fob as she's pointing to it in her hand. The higher ranking man nods. One of the marines, a younger man with a rather large pink X shaped scar on his right cheek, catches Cathode spying on them. He slightly raises an eyebrow at her. Cathode lets her spinning chair take her eyeline away from the marines.

As her chair comes to a stop in the opposite direction another scientist walks by and gives her a smirking friendly look. With her arms still raised straight up in the air Cathode gives a tiny wave of her hand.

"Morning, Mister Raman."

"Good morning, Miss Rei. Since you're obviously going to be around more please feel free to call me Thibodeaux."

"Tibble down?"

"Close. Tih bah dough. Thibodeaux."

"Oh, okay. Thibodeaux. Sorry, that's sort of a wild name. Like thermal, I mean. You can call me Catho- um... Catherine is fine."

"It's not very common. It's French in origin, actually. How you spell mine is the Cajun way. You know. The right way."

Thibodeaux smirks awkwardly, raising his eyebrows. Cathode blinks at him.

"That was a joke."

"Ah. Ha."

"Hey, don't worry about it. I'm told my sense of humor doesn't always translate well."

Cathode smirks back at Thibodeaux.

"Well, there we have something in common."

"Great! We can be awkward together."

Cathode chuckles with Thibodeaux. Bridget quietly walks up behind Cathode having concluded her business with the LF representative.

"I knew the work could be boring but I didn't think it was *that* boring."

Popping out of her chair to stand Cathode waves to Thibodeaux as he leaves and smugly leads Bridget to sit in her place.

"Oh, it's not *that* boring. My compiler is doing most of the heavy lifting anyway."

Bridget, concerned, sits down and spins the chair back to the terminal screen.

"Your what? You didn't install any additional software on this system did you? That's super duper against the rules."

"No! I know! I didn't install a single thing, I swear. I just wrote a simple compiler in the system to run the backup filing tasks. I still manually check output but it's built to take any files older than the threshold from the database and prep it for backup."

Watching the status percentage rise Bridget leans back in the chair.

"And you wrote this yourself?"

"Yup. Probably the third day I was here."

"Why didn't you say anything if it was this easy?"

"I didn't... I didn't want you to be mad at me for cheating the job."

Bridget stands up laughing loudly. She leads Cathode by the shoulder into the lab.

"I'm not mad! And that's definitely not cheating the job. If you'd told me earlier that you'd streamlined a bottleneck issue for our backups I could have put you on a secondary task."

Cathode lowers her head in shame. She bites her lower lip and looks up at her aunt.

"Sorry. I guess I'm just used to being punished for what most people consider cutting corners. What would my secondary task have been?"

"Your secondary task, which I'm giving you now, is to help me run diagnostics on the baseline systems inside the Superfluous."

Making a fist Cathode pulls it toward her body with a very quiet "yes" escaping her lips. Bridget smiles down at her niece. She reaches into her lab coat pocket and pulls out the ship's key fob. She dangles it in front of Cathode's face.

"Hop in."

Without a second thought Cathode snatches the key fob and clicks the bay unlock button. With a loud hiss the bottom hatch door begins to drop.

"Once you're in the co-pilot seat we'll start running very basic tests on the power systems."

"Thermal!"

Cathode doesn't wait for the hatch doors to fully open before leaping into the cargo hold. Just as she reaches the small ladder to the cockpit she spins around and rushes back out past Bridget. Bridget waits for the hatch door to finish opening before stepping up inside the cargo hold. Cathode rummages in her satchel bag. She pulls out Jeremy's card. She beams with pleasure as she passes Bridget again toward the cockpit ladder.

"What's that?"

"Oh, just a little reminder."

Entering the cockpit Cathode sits in the driver seat and places the little cup of noodle card off to the side of the dash display.

"Now. Let's get to work."

Bridget hands a diagnostic tablet and gets comfortable in the co-pilot seat.

"I said YOU in the co-pilot seat. But, yes, let's."

Biometrically logging in to the tablet Cathode flicks through a few menu systems.

"Hey, which system is Project Hou Yi? I saw it mentioned a few times in the earlier files for archival but it disappeared soon after. Was it renamed?"

Bridget adjusts, suddenly a bit uncomfortable in her seat, and looks sternly at Cathode.

"That project is classified. It's something... similar to the Superfluous but being run by a different division here. Best to just forget about it. Thank you for letting me know that it's mentioned in those files. I'm going to send Thibodeaux a message to move those to the right server."

Cathode fidgets in her chair momentarily.

"Did I screw up again?"

"Not at all, sweetie. You're doing your job almost too well."

Bridget chuckles and begins powering up the dash systems. Cathode relaxes and leans back in her chair, hugging her tablet to her chest.

Several hours later, Cathode hops out of the back of the Superfluous and clicks the hatch button. She puts the key fob in her pocket and walks over to Bridget's terminal.

"That is a whole lot of systems."

"Yes, but, thanks to you I now know it is 90% complete and could, in theory, be ready for a test flight."

"I volunteer to be a test dummy."

Bridget begins to close out her apps and shut down her terminal.

"Requires a bit higher clearance to be the test *pilot* for this ship. But, I sent in the request for a test next week so you'll be here if we do let it sail for a bit."

Cathode suddenly hugs Bridget around the waist, burying her face in Bridget's lab coat. Muffled, she lets out a wavering, "Thanks."

Bridget hugs her back and leans away so she can see Cathode's face.

"Don't mention it, sweetie."

Looking past Cathode, Bridget sees a small popup appear on Cathode's terminal.

"Looks like your friend... Boy. Ride is here to pick you up."

"You can call him Lazy."

"I wouldn't dream of it! He seems to be a very reliable, hard working young man."

Cathode tries not to laugh while still hugging Bridget.

"No... auntie, that's his nick."

"Ah. Well, pack up. I'll see you tomorrow."

Bridget gives Cathode a soft kiss on the crown of her head before peeling Cathode off of her. Cathode smiles warmly at her, then goes and shuts down her terminal.

“Is it just me or is that not just a big old rock?”

Lazy points past Cathode’s face toward the grayish tented structure outside the research facility as they are leaving. “I know I’ve only been driving this route a few weeks now but I noticed it after, like, the first week.”

“Yeah, I saw it earlier. Might be some sort of secondary ventilation system. I should ask my aunt about it tomorrow.”

Turning her attention back to the front of the cab Cathode sees a small pamphlet stuck in the center console tray. She picks it up as Lazy gets slightly flush in the face.

“What is this?”“Oh, uh, some guy at the mines handed that to me. Said he wanted the old delivery girl to have it. I was going to throw it away but thought maybe you’d get a laugh out of it.”

Flipping the pamphlet over Cathode sees it’s for the sun cult. She smirks. “He wanted me to have this? One of these dementos followed me a while ago. They seem to be getting everywhere.”

“Yeah, stupid right?”

“Yeah...”

Cathode is distracted by a tiny, seemingly tiny pixel print error on the pamphlet on the cult's logo. Cathode flips down her goggles and dials the side of her lenses to digitally zoom in on the error. It's actually a perfectly printed QR code. She takes a snapshot of the code.

"There's a QR code buried in this stupid logo."

"What does it bring up?"

"Hold on. Let me preload all my antivirus systems. Anti UP!"

A small line of green code scrolls up the left side of Cathode's vision. At one hundred percent load Cathode double taps the air in front of the QR code. Her web browser begins loading a site. It's a simple, mostly empty site with a single video player panel.

"Put the cart on auto drive for a sec. Let's see what this video is."

Tapping the steering wheel, which folds into the dashboard, Lazy leans back in his chair. Cathode makes a flick motion and the website loads onto the center console screen of the cab. She flips up her goggles and taps the large purple play button on the video. A man in a large bronze mask, with wavy sun rays shooting out of it, sits in a blackened room. The lower jaw of his mask moves in a robotic manner as he speaks in a dull drone.

"Illumination upon thee. I am Solis. High priest to the eternal light. You have fine eyes. And an inquisitive, brilliant mind. You searched for a light in the darkness and I am here to say you have indeed found it. Light that is life. The real deal. Pure energy."

Solis raises a hand to the camera. He lets his fingers dance in the spotlight illuminating one side of his shiny mask.

"The kind of energy that even a blind man can feel."

He lowers his hand and adjusts himself in his chair.

"But you know that. This hum. This hum through all of us. Passes through the universe. We feel it. You feel it now. You want to know where it comes from. Its origin. Now, you are thinking, here comes the pitch. Well, worry not. This is no secret to hide. Nor would I ever dream to obscure the truth from you. The answer is obvious too. Especially to one so clever. The sun, Sol, Helios. He is there in plain sight. No hidden deity. No magical phantom. Just pure life giving energy."

Lazy briefly glances at the sun.

"Helios is right there. But, a darkness has diminished that light. Humans travel further from it in a maddening frenzy into the darkness. Humans wish to become titans. Titans wished to be gods. But, even the gods fear Helios' true power. That, I see, is the truth. We are fleeing the maddening idea of rejoining the purity and exquisite energy of Helios. The men of Area are too far gone at this time. But, those of Geo and Selene can still bathe in the unfettered power. That is truly where you come in. You are a vessel of his energy, a lamp, who can spread your positivity to those still trapped in the darkness. Some will not want to come out of the dark as their work is evil. But, there is no darkness in pure light. We need to be, and amplify, our lamps. I can not do this alone and require lanterns like you. A cleansing is required. A commitment to the guardians of oaths. A faith in the radiance. A conviction to pull the chariot when needed. This is a selfless act to save all of humanity and bring us all back to nourishing radiance. This I ask of you. Help me. Help them. Help them all. Spread the truth. The light is truth. Help us all reconnect in the hum. Thank you. Illumination upon us all."

At the end of the video the man sits still as a simple exter-net email address sits on the screen in front of him. Lazy looks over at Cathode who looks a bit perplexed.

"That was... something, huh?"

"Something sure describes it. And you said the guy wanted me to have this pamphlet? Like, was I supposed to find that link? Is this how they recruit for real? The cleansing sounds threatening, right? This is super weird. I'm going to run an analyzer on it.

"Or, maybe, we could just forget about it and watch something more interesting."

"Yes, to the interesting thing. But hold on. Run video analytics three point five."

A slight hum sounds from Cathode's goggles as they begin to scrub the video for any type of details from reflections, sounds, metadata, or anything else that would let her know where the video was created.

"Alright, show me something interesting."

Lazy lowers his own goggles and flicks something to the center console screen. A film begins playing.

"So, what is this?"

"Ok, so... OK, so, I found this on an old data dump site that apparently was originally some earth aimed satellite's storage system. The movie has a bunch of crazy names but my favorite title for it is Aliennators."

"What?"

"Just watch."

On the screen a Gynoid in a metal bikini fires her arm cannon laser causing a truck to disappear in green light. Cathode adjusts in her seat and realizes she's had the ship's key fob this entire time.

"Crud."

"What?"

"I need to go back to work. I accidentally pocketed something."

"Accidentally?"

"Yes. Like a legitimate accident. Please, just turn around."

Lazy taps the steering wheel controls and sets a u-turn course back to the lab.

"I can just send you the film file. You don't have to make excuses to finish this piece of art."

"Har. Har. I really do need to go back. But, I will take this for the library later."

Lazy triggers the fence gate, takes control of the delivery vehicle and steers it into a parking space. Cathode pops on her helmet, slides up the face shield, and hops out of the cab. Slightly perplexed Lazy looks past her at a nearly identical looking delivery truck parked in the corner. As Cathode's walking to the door she sees Mr. Mitchell is staring intensely at her from behind his desk. Cathode raises her palm like a wave to show him she's got the key fob and just here to return it. His hands are palm flat on top of his desk. He slightly shakes his head at her and shifts his eyes to the far right of the room where Cathode can't currently see. She freezes but the automatic door hisses to life and opens.

"RUN!"

Mr. Mitchell yells at Cathode loud enough for her to hear it through her helmet as he suddenly ducks under his desk. The facility alarm claxons pop down out of the ceiling as Mr. Mitchell reappears with a large shotgun looking weapon. He points it at a growing shadow moving toward Cathode. He fires. It's so loud Cathode can hear the shot through her helmet. A splash of blood hits the wall in front of the automatic doors, splattering across the air in front of Cathode. Mr. Mitchell screams again as his body seems to twitch. Cathode is frozen for only a moment realizing Mr. Mitchell is being shot by several weapons. A helmeted head peeks around the corner at her. Cathode closes her grip on the key fob, pivots on her heels and leaps down to the floor of the parking structure. She runs at full speed toward Lazy in the delivery truck. She taps her helmet.

"Lazy! Guns! Go!"

Lazy looks out the passenger side window, sees Cathode charging toward him and reaches to flip open the passenger door. She jumps in as he peels backwards, almost ramming into a retaining wall. Cathode looks out the open passenger door back at a man, the helmeted head that peeked at her, in a tannish green full tactical military grade spacesuit and he wears a poncho over the whole suit that has the sun cult's logo emblazoned on it. Lazy takes a hard left as the man lifts a large assault rifle from under his poncho and fires a few rounds at the truck. The shots spray up the wall, barely missing, as Lazy cuts back around to the exit. The man does not give chase but casually walks back into the lab security room, free hand to his helmet.

"What was that?!"

Cathode shuts her door and sits back against her seat. She stares straight ahead. Her helmet is still on.

"I don't know! I don't know. I don't. I don't..."

Lazy pushes the truck to go faster. He quickly glances back at the lab in his rear view monitor. A small explosion rips open one side of the lab.

"Aunt Bridget... Lazy! The gate!"

"Oh shit!"

Lazy tries to cut around the gate but doesn't completely make it. The arm of the gate is almost obliterated from the grill on the truck. A large part of it smashes into the windshield causing a tiny chip. Cathode quickly grabs Lazy's helmet and locks it on his suit for him. The windshield splinters, cracks and oxygen shoots out of the larger holes. Lazy focuses straight ahead, pushing the truck to regain the speed it lost from the gate. Cathode checks the rearview monitor. A small low orbit skimmer ship lifts off from somewhere behind the lab's nearby crater lip. It shoots straight up and then hooks back down toward the surface headed directly at the delivery truck.

"Go. Faster!"

"I'm trying!"

The skimmer begins to close the gap between them. Lazy cuts onto a major highway filled with mining vehicles. Cathode flips down her goggles and loads the rearview monitor into an overlay. She watches in horror as the skimmer's underbelly unlocks revealing a rail gun barrel. The barrel begins to glow with the heat of the weapon preparing to fire.

"Left now!"

Lazy twists the wheel and shifts two lanes narrowly avoiding a small employee bus. The ground to the right of the bus explodes, sending shards of smart-crete across the road. Lazy attempts to wipe the sweat from his brow but just smacks his hand on his helmet's visor. Cathode brings up a map app and quickly starts tracking ahead of them. While also keeping an eye on the skimmer as it floats above them reloading. She looks forward to seeing a large overpass coming up.

"Cut across the median under the overpass."

"What?!"

"Just do it. Now!"

Lazy yanks the e-brake handle, spins the wheel and aims down into the ditch median between the two sides of the highway. The little delivery truck pops up on the other side into oncoming traffic. Lazy turns right into that oncoming traffic as the top of the overpass explodes from a second shot from the skimmer.

A midsize truck falls through the opening and crashes next to Lazy as he floors the accelerator again. He drives straight toward one of the massive mine dump trucks. It blasts its horn. The skimmer spirals backwards around the destroyed overpass, down to nearly road level and picks up the chase. Cathode sees what he's doing. She quickly brings up an app marked as wireless control.

"Go straight!"

"I- Oh no..."

Working as quickly as possible Cathode overrides the dump truck's controls and locks the steering straight. The driver of the truck frantically tries to turn the wheel and jam on the brakes according to Cathode's app. The skimmer's rail gun looks to be heating up again. Lazy grits his teeth and squints his eyes shut as they drive directly under the middle of the dump truck. Cathode taps hopper control and pauses for a brief moment, checking that the skimmer has decided to chase directly behind them. She taps for the hopper to drop just as the delivery truck clears the back of the dump truck. The massive bed of the dump truck immediately tilts up from behind the cab and dumps its load of rock onto the road. The skimmer has no time to react and explodes underneath the truck. Cathode stops the dump truck and returns control to the driver. She lets out a sigh of relief. Lazy still has a deathgrip on the wheel. Noticing the skimmer's explosion he wheels right and steers the truck back across the median to the proper side. Only once they've been safely driving for a few minutes does he loosen his grip and sit back. He glances over at Cathode, who looks equally exhausted.

"What is happening?"

"I still don't know. Let's just get-"

The roadway in front of the delivery truck explodes, the truck hits the destroyed smart-crete and flies several feet into the air before slamming back to the road. Cathode loads the rearview monitor back up in her goggles. She doesn't see anything. Lazy taps her shoulder and points out her window as a second skimmer zips across the road in front of them. At the extreme speed it's going the skimmer is forced to start a wide arc to get back toward them. Lazy cracks his knuckles by flexing his grip on the steering wheel as he maneuvers the delivery truck to hide behind a large maintenance van. The skimmer has almost lined up behind them when it suddenly spins off. Two Lunar Frontiersmen vehicles, lights and sirens screaming come down out of seemingly empty space and give chase to the skimmer. Cathode and Lazy watch as the chase weaves away from them. A third skimmer rockets past them to join the fight. Cathode reaches out to grip Lazy's shoulder.

"Get us home."

Lazy pushes the engine to its maximum and heads toward the exit for the Aristarchus crater entrance. Cathode watches in horror as one of the LF vehicles bursts into flames as the third skimmer is able to land a shot on its tail section. The LF's pilot escape pod flies off just in the nick of time. The second LF vehicle continues to chase the second skimmer in a dizzying zigzagging dog fight. Lazy skids to a stop next to a small group of vehicles that are waiting inside the lock for the exit airlock to close. The door slowly shuts as Cathode and Lazy watch the rearview monitor. The second LF ship spirals down into the ground and explodes. There is no escape pod. Both skimmers cut sharp turns and head toward them. They both let out sighs of relief as the massive exit airlock securely closes and the interior opens. They quickly skip ahead of the line. As the truck goes over the interior door's lip the walls rattle like an earthquake hit them. Dust and rocks fall from the ceiling. One of the skimmers took a shot at the exterior door. More emergency claxons go off and the interior door quickly goes into a safety closure. Lazy pushes the small truck in front of them out of the way narrowly avoiding the interior door taking off their back bumper. The car behind them reverses in order to avoid being crushed by the massive door. Lazy weaves around the truck he hit and waves his arms, looking like a crazy person, at the driver. The driver looks mad for a brief moment before peeling off toward the vehicle elevators. Lazy quickly cuts around a slow vehicle toward the center of the parking level. Another explosion rocks the entire structure. The very air in the parking structure shifts and funnels like a tornado up and out toward the Forest level. Cathode looks up in horror.

"They blasted the dome open!"

"What! IS! HAPPENING?!"

The dome begins its emergency iris shutter closure due to the rail gun rupture. One skimmer makes it through the shattered opening before the shutter closes. The other is not as lucky and smashes into the closed shutter. With a second shot the surviving skimmer blows a hole in the bottom of the lake at the center of the Forest level. Lazy skids around the central opening of Storage as a deluge of water from the burst lake blasts down into the city. Cathode looks up to see the skimmer's nosecone emerging from within the now dwindling waterfall. It comes to a near dead halt at their level and fires. The shot burns a line across the truck's hood and explodes inside the vehicle elevator Lazy was headed toward. He spins the wheel around. Cathode loads her collision and trajectory clairvoyance apps.

"What do we do?"

"Drive at him. Straight. Fast."

"Wha-"

"Now!"

Lazy stomps the accelerator one last time. He twists the wheel and steers right back for the open center of Storage that connects all levels of the crater. The skimmer adjusts, floating in the middle opening with two cultists inside, tracking them. Its rail gun begins to glow again. Inside Cathode's goggles she sees a red wireframe layout of the city, the truck they are in and several lines of code doing real time equations.

"When do I turn?!"

Lazy steals a quick side eye glance at Cathode, terror on his pale face. Everything begins flashing inside Cathode's helmet. A dotted trajectory line appears falling into the wireframe city.

"Now! Left!"

Cathode reaches over and pulls the truck's e-brake. The skimmer's railgun fires just as the truck twists sideways. The truck slams into a security barrier a few feet from the opening causing it to go into a quick aileron roll. The railgun shot goes under the truck, technically over its now upside down roof, and the truck smashes into the skimmer's cockpit. Both vehicles drop like stones through the central opening. Cathode's goggles begin flashing new dotted lines that end in

"X"-es all over the city. Lazy looks down to see the entire city seemingly not getting any closer to them. Cathode releases the e-brake and looks out as well. The entire city is in fact sinking as the security measures for a dome rupture cause all buildings to recede under the ground. Essentially becoming bunkers until repairs allow livable conditions again, if ever. Cathode sees the XiLaYu building, the largest in the city, beneath them. Its steepled roof has no flat area on top of it. In her goggles the building isn't moving. The program didn't take that into consideration. The truck continues it's sideways rotation. Cathode loses sight of the building top but can see the red outline in her goggles as she looks at the floor of the truck cab.

"Put it in reverse!"

The truck slams, rear wheels first, into the top of the XiLaYu building roof and skids down towards the edge. A damaged tire bursts as the truck attempts to pull backward from the roof's lip. Lazy checks the rearview monitor just in time to see the skimmer's shadow. He twists the wheel to the right as the skimmer slams into the roof right next to Cathode's door. It's empty. The pilot and co-pilot ejected before impact. Cathode's goggles flash a new trajectory. She moves her head to align it.

"Punch it! Forward!"

Lazy shifts into drive and tries to keep the truck on the slanted roof edge.

"There's nothing there!"

"Just do it! Trust me!"

Lazy focuses as the delivery truck continues to skid sideways, crunching over shrapnel from the skimmer, trying to keep it going straight. He flinches as they break through a small guardrail and sail over the edge of the roof. Cathode grips onto her seatbelt as they fly out into nothing. The truck comes to a quick crashing halt, breaking the front axle and throwing the windshield's empty frame over the edge of the shorter Girisha-go building's roof. Cathode lets out a long exhale. She blinks her eyes a few times and closes her apps. She looks over at Lazy. He's broken the truck's steering wheel. His hands are still gripping the top piece that broke off. Cathode taps his shoulder. He suddenly inhales, drops the steering wheel piece into his lap and screams. Cathode unbuckles and gets out of the truck. Lazy follows in a partial daze. As the whole city sinks into the ground Cathode opens a roof security door. Lazy looks back at the destroyed truck as Cathode heads inside.

“I’m so fired...”

Glancing up Lazy sees the shadowy shapes of the cultists’ ejector seats approaching the roof. He quickly shuts the security door, locks it and rushes down the stairs with Cathode.

Cathode reaches the fifth floor of the building, the level that links as an airlock into all the other bunker systems, and waits for a moment. The city is still sinking and locking in so the bunker network hasn't cleared any airlocks just yet. Lazy sits down on the stairs behind her and removes his helmet. He sits frozen for a moment. Cathode also removes her helmet and adjusts her goggles. Lazy tilts his head slowly up toward Cathode.

"What the hell was that?!"

"I don't- I don't know."

The claxon lights in the building shift from red to orange as the building hits its lock-in point and the airlock door controls flicker to life. Cathode taps on the controls and air rushes out of the airlock door as it opens. A door slams somewhere above them. Lazy's eyes dart from the door to the ceiling.

"More?"

"Time to go."

Lazy passes Cathode into the bunker airlock. As she turns to enter, Cathode swings her helmet and smashes the outer controls. The sound of footsteps echo on the stairs as Lazy closes the door. After a beat a chime sounds and the bunker tunnel side airlock door slides open. There are signs on the walls of the tunnel for the subway system. It becomes the emergency hallways in case of dome breach. Cathode and Lazy rush down the hallway. The walls in the hallway are all display screens showing a general warning of a dome breach. A distraught news caster appears on the video walls as they continue into the bunker system.

"Aristarchus has been breached by unknown terrorists. The dome emergency seal has closed. The mayor's office recommends all citizens remain inside the bunkers and within a safe distance from emergency oxygen masks. The Lunar Frontiersmen have been mobilized. Please remain calm and-"

The video feed cuts out for a moment. With the screens blacked out Lazy stumbles. Cathode helps him up as a metallic pounding echoes behind them. Whoever came down the stairs made it to the airlock and are attempting to break it open. A technical difficulties image appears on the wall screens. Cathode turns on her goggles to their AR setting and loads a map overlay of where all the emergency bunker hallways go. She looks around in a large arc.

"We take this right and then two lefts to get to the main mall bunker cell. There should be other people there."

"Great. As long as that door behind us holds."

Taking the second left, Cathode taps the airlock in front of them and they enter through it into a massive room filled with terrified shoppers from the Yueguang Mall. Back down the hallway they came from, a muffled explosion goes off, further terrifying the shoppers huddled inside the bunker room. Cathode and Lazy carefully weave into the crowd to get away from the airlock door. The room wall video displays all turn on with a handheld camera feed looking at a dirty floor. The camera tilts up and Cathode freezes in her tracks almost knocking Lazy to the ground again. On the screens Solis, dressed in an elaborate golden spacesuit version of his outfit from the hidden video, stands in Aunt Bridget's lab with a small group of the scientist and workers on their knees behind him. Bridget is at the end of the line. Solis addresses the camera directly.

"People of the galaxy. Greetings. My name is Solis. The high stoic priest to the eternal light of Helios. We have taken control of all feeds on the lunar surface. And several of the externet as well. The human race has lost the light. The path has darkened. These people behind me have created a device that will help return us all to the purity. This was not my planned way to introduce you all to the future. But, we needed to reach out because one of them... These brilliant, but misguided people. One of them has taken the key to the future. The brightness continues to dim. We can not simply ask for the key. We know it will not be returned without a force of darkness. So, to you, whoever you are, bring us back our key to the light and save us all."

Solis steps back from the camera. He holds out his hand and a similarly dressed cultist hands him a handgun. Solis takes it, checks the chamber and aims it at Thibodeaux.

"Hurry and return it to us. Or they will all suffer the same fate."

Solis presses the barrel of the gun to the back of Thibodeaux's head. He grits his teeth before screaming at the camera.

"DON'T GIVE IT TO-"

Solis fires. Cathode lets loose an inhuman scream as every video wall shows Thibodeaux's dead body fall backwards. The terrified crowd wails in terror. Lazy catches Cathode who seems ready to faint.

"Cathode?!"

Margaret pushes through the crowd nearest to Cathode.

"What are you doing here? What is happening? Is this real?"

Cathode crumples to the ground as Lazy and Margaret squat next to her. On the video screen Solis steps up to the next scientist in the line. He pauses, tapping the gun against his hip. He turns to the camera.

"That was unfortunate. We had hoped to just be on our way without a fuss. Best hurry, little light. There will not be many left."

The mall security bunker room goes dark again before the technical difficulties image reappears. Adults and children all over the room begin to cry.

Cathode gives a weak nod to Margaret and timidly reaches into her pocket. She pulls out the key fob to the Superfluous and looks at it. Cathode is deathly pale. Lazy looks at it in shock.

"That's the key?"

Lazy realizes how loud he just was and leans in to whisper to the girls.

"The thing they're looking for? What is it for?"

Margaret hooks her arm under Cathode's and helps her stand. Lazy does the same and they begin to slowly walk through the crowd to a less populated area. Cathode's eyes don't leave the key fob.

"Yeah. Yes. I think. I mean, it has to be. But it's just a device to unlock the ship. Why do they need the ship? Why... Why is this happening?"

Lazy looks at the key fob and then slowly scans the room.

"I don't know about any of this. But, whatever they want it for they want it bad. We definitely can't stay here if they're coming for it."

Margaret lets Cathode lean against a table near the back of the room.

"I am so lost."

Cathode finally looks Margaret in the eyes.

"Margaret? Why are you here? Where did you come from?"

"I was shopping with my mom and then the lockdown alarms all went off so we got into the main mall elevator and... that doesn't matter. What is any of this?! That was your aunt next to the guy who got shot. This can't be real."

Lazy curls his shoulders forward and sighs.

"It's very real. Those cultists chased us here. They blew out the dome trying to get that key thingy. I know only a little more than you."

Cathode slows her breathing for a moment. Closing her eyes she centers her mind.

"We need to get the ship out of there. They'll just keep coming for it. That's all I've got right now. Thibodeaux had to have known I have the key fob. He would have asked Bridget. Oh no! Bridget!"

Lazy seems to have blanked out, staring at the ground. He blinks a few times. Margaret looks back and forth between them, seeming to panic.

"You can't be serious! Give that key thing to the LF."

Cathode puts the key fob back in her pocket and zips it shut

"They won't be able to get in quickly with the dome emergency iris shut. We'll have to go to them. Lazy, we know the cult is at the ship already. We get there and we can trade it for the hostages. At least stall until the LF can show up.

Something... anything to keep them alive. I just don't know how we get back to the lab with the truck destroyed on that roof."

Margaret's jaw goes slack listening to Cathode calmly ramble her plan out. Lazy rubs his gloved hands together, slightly trembling as the adrenaline of the vehicle chase drains away.

"If you think that'll save the remaining hostages then I'm in."

"Good. Now, it's just a matter of how."

Out of the corner of his eye Lazy sees the airlock door they entered from open. Two cultists enter holding assault rifles. The crowd begins to panic even before one shoots into the ceiling.

"Everybody down!"

Most of the crowd begins to push back against the walls or drop to the floor immediately. Cathode, Margaret and Lazy all duck down but remain on their feet. Lazy gently pushes the girls toward the nearest airlock door.

"We can worry about the how later. We need to get out of here now."

Margaret lets them pass her as they reach the door.

"I'll slow them down."

Cathode opens her mouth to argue but Margaret shakes her head. With her left hand Margaret quickly taps on her inner right wrist. The glow of her embedded cybernetic control system display shifts from green to red.

"They'll kill you if they catch you here. You've got to go. Now. GUN! MOVE!"

Margaret's scream makes the nearby shoppers scramble to their feet and rush into the middle of the room. Using the distraction Margaret hits the airlock control to open. She pushes them both inside as it slides open. Using her strength amplified right hand Margaret crushes the controls and steps in with them. The airlock quickly closes as the cultists head toward the center of the room pushing the panicking people down.

"Come with us Margaret."

"I'll be fine. You don't have to worry about me. Really."

Lazy opens the exterior airlock door and grabs Cathode's arm to pull her out. Margaret nods to him. He weakly smiles back. As they turn to leave, Margaret gouges her fingers into a side wall and easily rips off a metal panel. As the exterior door shuts she jams the panel into the locking mechanism so the door can't fully close causing the entire system to malfunction. She turns around to look through the airlock window. The cultists have reached the door. They look at her, the broken door control and then past Margaret. Smiling, Margaret slowly raises her right hand, her middle finger extended. One of the cultists points his rifle at her but the other grabs the barrel and lowers it. They turn, as the crowd parts to avoid them, and head toward another airlock.

Lazy and Cathode are in a light sprint heading down hallways. Cathode is looking through walls with her mapping system but she doesn't see anything useful.

"I've got nothing. I don't know where to go. We need a vehicle. We need to get out. Need to-"

Thibodeaux.

Trying to lean against the wall Cathode collapses, sliding down it and sobbing.

"They killed him. Like it was nothing. And Brodin. And they still have Bridget."

Lazy quickly kneels next to her and hugs her. His eyes flash with a sudden realization.

"My bike."

"What?"

"My bike. We take my old float-bike."

Cathode opens her AR iris and wipes the tears out of her eyes.

"What? Wait, that thing you had when you were, like, nine?"

"Yeah, remember how I was going to run away from home? At some point after the funeral... anyway, I parked it outside that one emergency exit after we had the elementary school safety tour of the bunkers. I never could get back outside to pick it up. Kind of just forgot about it. Until now."

Lazy helps Cathode to her feet.

"You think it will make it?"

"Battery might be shot but I had a solar charge sail attachment in the saddle bag. It's the best I can offer. Otherwise we've got to walk to the next city. Right?"

Cathode considers it for a moment.

"Best shot we've got. It was the southern school emergency exit right? I think we're not too far from that."

"Okay. Let's go."

Cathode taps her AR iris closed again and maps out the directions to that exit. She sees a note icon with a "!" on it on her menu. She opens it as they walk. Margaret sent her a message, "They went off to the west exit. You should have time to get wherever you're going. They don't know that loops back through the downtown bunkers. I ripped the door open and I'm with my mom. We're safe. Be safe. Respond when you are as well. - Manticore"

A small smile spreads across Cathode's lips. Lazy kneels next to an exterior exit airlock covered in faded warnings about dangers and fines for opening it. He types something in the air in front of his helmeted face for his goggle's input. He chuckles nervously.

"They never updated the security systems on these things. I'm literally still in here as an anonymous user access account from over six years ago. That's actually kind of terrifying. Security wise. If everything else wasn't so insane right now maybe I'd be able to properly process- Got it."

With a groan and a creaky hiss the airlock door stutters open. Cathode steps into the airlock while relocking the neck of her helmet. She nods to Lazy when it clicks shut and he triggers the exterior door. A fine powder of dust is blasted out onto the surface of the moon. Lazy and Cathode's goggles both trigger their UV filters as the near blinding reflection of the Sun's light on the lunar surface shines into the airlock bay. Lazy hesitantly steps out onto the surface as the dust cloud continues floating out, slowly beginning to settle. The area seems as dead as any other unprotected place on the moon. Lazy turns and looks to the top of the organic outer rim of the crater. He can just barely make out the external emergency lights for the city. He turns to his right and walks down the crater wall to a large craggy outcropping. Cathode pats the key fob through her suit. Her eyes drop to the ground, staring at nothing in particular. Lazy reaches into a crevice in the outcropping and slowly, carefully pulls a dust and rock covered tarp out. Pulling the tarp away he reveals a blue-ish gray kids sized hoverbike. He taps the cartoonishly large red switch on the top of the front hover plate. The screen on the handlebars chirps to life and immediately begins flashing an empty battery icon. The screen intermittently flashes the words “open solar sails for recharge“. Lazy reads the words upside down and taps the screen. The solar sails rod pops up from the saddle bag on the back hover plate’s frame. The solar sails unfurl, jut forward and snap together into a triangular shape, like a hang glider, almost chopping Lazy in the throat. He takes a startled step back and realizes the small sails mean they both have to sit hunched for the entire trip. Cathode comes up behind him.

“I thought it was pearl blue?”

“Cheap paint. Faded over the years. apparently, even under a tarp. I’ll be sure to write the company a strongly worded E.M. about it later.”

The battery indicator continues to flash red as one of the five charge bars fills. Lazy gently leans against the crater wall. Cathode’s eyes drift upward into the void. Lazy follows her gaze.

“Did you... do you want... I mean, I can listen. Or not.”

Cathode blinks a few times. She looks to Mars for a moment and then over at Lazy.

“Not right now. Let’s just get the key fob to the lab.”

Lazy looks up at the stars as well for a moment. He nods softly and looks back to the hover bike’s battery icon turns yellow as a second bar fills.

“Should be able to run while continuing to charge now without an issue.”

Lazy unlatches the center of the bike’s frame allowing it to be extended, design wise for taller children, but in this case so there is a larger seat area for both of them. He locks the extension in place, slides his leg over the seat and pats behind him as he scoots forward. Cathode awkwardly squeezes in behind him and grips around his curled waist as he powers up the bike. It lets out an audible whine as the hover plates hum with power. The bike floats only an inch off the ground. Lazy taps the screen and sets the child weight from thirty one kilograms to sixty five. The bike whines again and then lurches over a foot off the ground.

Lazy kicks his foot off the crater wall to push the bike out. He twists the throttle causing the back hover plate to rotate backwards to a seventy five degree angle as it begins to propel the bike forward.

As the tiny bike reaches the edge of the security fence Cathode peeks over Lazy's shoulder. The entire lab is still in lockdown. She points out the vent and Lazy nods. They skim off behind a dune to avoid detection and curve around to the vent edge. It's actually larger than Lazy thought. Its size makes it more apparent that the vent is not just for venting the atmosphere from the lab safely, it's also an emergency escape tunnel system. Lazy slows the hover bike and Cathode leaps off. She rushes over to the disguised airlock and finds the control pad. She flips open the pad's cover and quickly punches in a code. Lazy flips the kickstand on the bike and hops off. Cathode is waiting for him as the airlock door opens.

"How did you know the code?"

"My aunt let it slip that her general access code was my mom's birthday."

"Oh, wow... Good thing it wasn't my mom's. I can't remember it. I mean, her birthday... that quickly."

Stepping in Cathode punches the close button and shakes her head at Lazy.

"You should probably work on that."

"I know. I know. Bad brain thing. Can't remember birthdays and names when I first meet someone. But, I can sure remember a vert jingle from fifty years ago."

As the interior airlock begins to open Cathode recklessly squeezes her way out and runs down the subterranean corridor headed to the lab. She brings up the still streaming live feed in her goggles. Solis is standing with his gun still on Bridget's head. Suddenly, a blast rocks the entire facility. Solis has a brief flash of looking scared and fires. Cathode collapses in the corridor screaming. Lazy runs up and puts his hands on her shoulder. She catches her chest and realizes Solis has fired past Bridget's face at something behind the camera operator. In the video stream the view quickly twists in a hundred and eighty degrees to a door of the lab as it explodes in. One of the two doors flies directly into the camera operator and the camera falls to the floor showing Solis rushing with his group to the back exit firing back at the unseen forces. Two surviving hostages are dragged out but Cathode isn't sure who they are.

Lazy helps Cathode stand up. She's transfixed on the video in her goggles. Lazy taps his own goggles to enlarge the same feed as the LF forces rush forward, shooting at the escaping cultists. It's a small battalion of LF marines and they quickly take control of the facility. A cultist charges back into the room. He's wearing a large vest of gray cubes with a red cord running to his hand. Cathode has never seen a real suicide vest before, but she knows immediately what it is. As the cultist takes a shot to the shoulder he twists sideways into a lab wall and explodes. The camera slides on the floor toward the massive hole blown in the wall as the room's atmosphere vents into space. The LF marines closest to the hole slam their heels on the floor activating their magne-boots. They continue to stomp after the remaining cultists. Thibodeaux's lifeless body slides out of the blasted hole behind them. A commander steps in behind the main force and begins ordering the closest men near him to search the lab for survivors and any other cultists. Cathode and Lazy continue down the corridor as the commander leans over the camera and kills the feed.

"We need to get those marines the key fob. They need to keep it safe. They can negotiate. I can't let Bridget down. I need to keep her safe. I need to."

"Ok. We'll get it to them. Let's just be careful. Some of those cultists might have come down here."

That makes Cathode pause for a moment. She hadn't thought of that. She shakes off her fear and continues forward. Cautiously, Cathode opens an airlock door that is hidden in the back wall of the security office. The airlock is disguised behind a corner wall panel. It silently shuts behind them. Cathode leans over the desk and flicks on the monitors for the security cameras. Her and Lazy watch as the commander rounds up every marine, except for two, they quickly rush back to their attack ship to give chase to the fleeing cultists. One of the marines helps the remaining three hostages get to an ambulance ship that is landing in front of the lab. Cathode and Lazy rush out to the remaining marine in the lab. The hostages' faces are all covered by emergency oxygen masks. Cathode and Lazy throw their hands up as they approach. The marine turns, shocked, aiming his rifle at them. The marine taps his helmet to set his communications system to the public channel. He lowers his gun. Through his visor Cathode recognizes his x shaped scar. He was one of the marines that had been here before.

"Where did you come from? It's not safe here. Especially for children. Wait, I know you..."

Cathode approaches the Superfluous slowly. She notices the blood streaks from where Thibodeaux's body was laying. She also realizes that the two people closest to Thibodeaux were the ones dragged away by the cultists.

"We had to come back. We brought the key fob for the ship. See."

Cathode reveals she has the key fob in her hand and taps the unlock button. The Superfluous chirps and the back hatch opens with its familiar hiss. Inside the cargo bay there is a giant black metal egg. Cathode pauses, confused, and stares at it. Lazy watches as the marine smiles behind his helmet's visor.

"Solis will be ecstatic."

"What?"

Cathode spins around as the marine raises his rifle at her.

"Give me the device! Helios demands it."

Lazy rips a monitor off the desk near him and throws it at the marine. It connects with his helmet but his magne-boots keep his feet on the floor. The marine bends in an awkward shape and screams. He twists his rifle over his chest to aim at Lazy and fires a burst. Lazy dives behind some refrigeration tanks that burst with cold fog plumes. The jets of fog swirl around the lab. Cathode takes the distraction to kick a wheeled metal cart into the marine breaking his hand and sending his rifle across the floor. Lazy charges forward and scoops it up. Cathode waves him into the Superfluous hatch as the marine turns off his magne-boots and flops to the floor in pain. He taps his helmet again to send a message.

"They have it. These kids have the key. They brought it back. It's here. In the ship. Project Hou Yi! The bomb! Solis! Come back quickly!"

Lazy hops into the cargo bay and looks from the marine to the bomb sitting a few feet from where he's standing.

"Hou Yi? ...Bomb?"

Cathode powers up the ship causing Lazy to almost fall out the back.

"Close the hatch!"

Lazy braces against the inner cargo bay wall as Cathode lifts the ship off and aims it toward the hole caused by the explosion.

"I don't know how!"

Cathode powers the engines and the ship launches out of the hole. Lazy is uncomfortable watching the bomb jiggles on it's bracers as Cathode hooks the Superfluous up into the space above the lab. Lazy uses his free hand to scan the marine's communication broadcast system. His goggle system finds the marine, public and cult channels. He taps the cult channel and sends it to Cathode's goggles as they fly. Over the channel they hear a bunch of chatter as Solis is ecstatic, while still being chased away by the marine attack ships. He sends two more skiffs to get the bomb.

"Destroy the ship for all I care. But save the bomb no matter what."

Lazy looks out the open back of the ship and sees the two skiffs already rushing toward them.

"Cathode, we've got company!"

Cathode shifts in her seat and aims the ship down toward the moon surface. She twists the ship in a corkscrew as the skiffs catch up and take some warning shots at them. Lazy, unlocks the cultist marine's rifle's safety controls and raises it with his free hand. The closest skiff matches the speed of the Superfluous and tries to side swipe into them. The skiff is a much smaller craft so it only rattles the Superfluous. But, it causes the bomb to hop in its supports. Lazy fires a burst of shots into the skiff's back engine block. The engine bursts into flames, devouring the pilot's oxygen, causing the skiff to spiral off and smash down onto the lunar surface. The second skiff smashes into the other side of the ship. The bomb bounces again. Lazy leans out and fires again. But his shots do no visible damage to the skiff as it curves back away. Holding his breath to aim, Lazy is about to fire as the skiff smashes into the Superfluous, hard. He is thrown into the bomb, dropping the rifle out the back. The bomb begins to slide down the hatch's bottom door. Lazy dives for it, triggering his magne-boots and attempts to palm the front of the bomb like a basketball. The smoothness of the metal makes it impossible in his gloves and the bomb slips out of his hands and out of the ship. He stares in disbelief as it slowly tumbles toward the surface. Seeing it fall out, the skiff slows.

"Oh! Oh no! Oh NO! NO NO NO NO!"

Cathode watches the rear camera on the control panel monitor. She sees it's empty and Lazy hanging out the back by his boots. Lazy doesn't move as he watches the bomb tumble.

"Go. Go faster! Go much faster! Now!"

Cathode taps through a menu system and transfers power more power into the engines. The ship rattles slightly as she pulls back on the throttle and the Superfluous launches up away from the moon. Lazy pushes himself up to standing. He stares straight forward as he is now standing completely horizontal to the lunar surface. The bomb slams into the surface. A massive cloud of dust bursts out from the impact. Lazy braces himself and closes his eyes. He winces.

Nothing happens.

"Lazy?! What happened?"

Lazy slowly opens his eyes, ever so slightly, and sees the dust cloud dissipating around the bomb impact crater. Lazy taps his goggles to zoom in his view of the impact crater. The remaining cult skiff lands next to it. The bomb is completely intact.

"Nothing. It wasn't activated, or whatever it needed to explode."

"That's fantastic!"

Lazy watches as the skiff pilot hops out and drags a hoverpad lift over to the bomb. The Superfluous travels further away from the moon quickly.

"Yes. But, no. It's not. They have it now."

Cathode sighs. The last thing Lazy can make out at a thousand times magnification is the cultist floating the bomb on the hoverpad lift into the skiff. Lazy blinks and the moon is now a tiny dot in space.

"Whoa. What happened? How fast are we going?"

Cathode checks the controls.

"I don't. We're going..."

Cathode does a quick calculation in her head.

"Somewhere near, like, one fifteenth light speed. But, that's impossible."

Lazy cautiously steps up the small ladder rungs leading from the cargo hold to the front cockpit. As he sits down in the co-pilot seat he taps a large button on the dash and the hatch door shuts. Cathode looks at him with pure sadness and regret.

"Uh, lucky guess... I should have shut it earlier. But, yeah, we are going crazy fast. We're almost about to reach Venus' orbital path."

"Please. Stop."

"I've been slowing down for almost, like, five minutes now. If we tried to dead stop right now the ship might not handle it. I'll try when it's safe. Seat Belts."

Cathode palms the key fob for a moment before placing it in a pouch on the center console. As Lazy puts on his seat belt a panel on the dash flashes and Cathode pushes down the throttle.

"Hold on."

The ship rattles as the main rear thrusters turn off and the reverse thrusters kick on. There is a screech from the exterior of the hull as something shakes loose. Both Cathode and Lazy are thrown into their seatbelts as the ship ramps its reverse thrusters to full power. Cathode looks out the front display as the larger of the ship's two rings floats out in front of them, it being the something that broke loose. A new warning message pops up on the center console. Cathode quickly reads "Stabilize exit ring?" and taps "Yes". Lazy and Cathode watch as mini thrusters on the exit ring correct it's position in space so it's perfectly presented to the Superfluous. The ship finally comes to a complete stop.

"What is that?"

"It's the exit ring."

Lazy clicks off his seatbelt and floats out slightly toward the forward display.

"That doesn't help. What is it the exit to?"

"The entrance ring."

"Okay! Seriously!"

"Sorry, sorry. It's just all this adrenaline. It's crazy. My arms are shaking. How can people want to do chems that mimic this feeling?"

"I know. It's like my heart wants to vomit out of my chest. So, what is that thing really?"

"It's the exit ring to the entrance ring that is still attached to the ship. When we fly into the entrance ring we fly out wherever the exit ring is."

In complete weightlessness Lazy uses his pointer finger to tap the glass of his helmet and then flicks his finger across the display screen sending his body into a slow spinning rotation. Cathode clicks out of her seatbelt and smiles as realization spreads across Lazy's face.

"Did you... did you just describe a teleportation system?"

"Yes! I KNOW RIGHT?!"

Lazy slaps out with both hands to stop his rotation. He's upside down to Cathode.

"Really? Really?! Holy Shi-"

"YES!"

"Does it?!"

"I don't know!"

Cathode is shaking her fists. She's so happy Lazy gets it. He claps his hands together. They both take a deep breath and talk at the same time.

"We need to test it!"

They nod at each other in agreement. They twist and contort back into their seats and re-clasp their seatbelts. Cathode brings up the main systems on the console. She swipes to send the menu information to both hers and Lazy's goggles. They quickly start scanning through the information as if in a race. Cathode is the first to tap the menu.

"Got it."

"I, as well."

"You need to-"

"Oh, I know."

Cathode smirks at Lazy. She flicks through the menu to set the exit ring to charge. Lazy uses a side panel to start charging the entrance ring system. Cathode engages the reverse thrusters.

"We should probably get a little bit of distance."

Lazy starts to look nervous.

"Right. But, what is the, uh, range on these things?"

Cathode smiles.

"I have no idea."

"Oh... Oh, good."

Lazy sits up and adjusts his seatbelt's tautness.

"For a real test we should be going in the opposite direction."

Cathode purses her lips for a moment and then nods in agreement. She flicks the flight stick to the side and the Superfluous spins away from the exit ring.

"How fast do we need to be going? Don't say eighty eight miles per hour."

Lazy with a blank expression looks from Cathode, to his menu and back to her.

"I was not going to say that. But, uh, close. It says we need to be going at a minimum of eighty three miles per hour. Wait. What? How can it be so slow?"

"You only need to pass the length of the ship through the rings in a second. How fast do you think you'd need to go to do that? Also, if I'm remembering correctly the entrance ring is also moving opposite the ship so it barely has to move to go through. The speed is mostly so when the ship exits it moves away from the rings they can recouple safely."

"I'm just- I'm just shocked you could hide something this thermal this long."

"I know. I'm proud of myself too."

The charge counters on the entrance ring hit one hundred percent. A few moments later the exit ring counters complete as well. Lazy checks the menu system one more time.

"That's it. That's it?"

Cathode checks the menu herself.

"Yup. That's it. So, let's just get it going here. Now. Going. Here we go."

Cathode hand floats over the throttle. Lazy looks at her with a similar look of fear.

"Do you trust your Aunt Bridget?"

"What? Yes, of course."

"Then, uh, let'er rip?"

Cathode stifles a chuckle and grips the throttle. She gives it a small push. The ship begins moving forward. Cathode takes a few deep breaths and flips the menu to "Activate Rings". She taps it. Lazy watches a screen of a rear facing ship camera as the exit ring lights up with energy. The interior of the ring seems to ripple briefly. Cathode takes one final deep breath, holds it, taps "Launch Entrance Ring". Just outside the hull of the ship, mechanisms push the entrance ring forward as its own thrusters launch it several yards in front of the Superfluous. They see the same rippling shimmer appear in the center of the entrance ring. Lazy tenses up and grips down on the chair's armrests as the entrance rings reverse thrusters fire and flies straight back at them. Both flinch but nothing happens. The stars in the front display bleed and blend into a new arrangement almost instantaneously. Cathode exhales and pulls the throttle to stop.

"Did it- did we- did it work?"

"I think so?"

Lazy releases his grip from armrests and pats his chest. He looks down at the rear camera display. He sees the smaller entrance ring appear inside the exit ring and then both latch together.

"Yes."

"Yes?"

"Yes. I'm looking at the two rings combining behind us and the Sun was at the rear of the ship a few seconds ago."

Cathode looks at the rear camera display and sees the two rings slightly adjusting their angle as they move to reconnect to the Superfluous. The same mechanisms that launched the entrance ring grab on again and lock the whole system onto the hull. Lazy stares at Cathode for a moment. They both blink, take a long breath in, and then fling their arms out. Cathode eyes almost escape their sockets; she's so excited.

"WE TELEPORTED!"

"WE DID! WE TELEPORTED!" They both shout out loud. Cathode takes another deep breath and relaxes against her seatbelt. She taps a few systems and nods.

"That sure happened."

"It sure did."

The dash display flashes with a transmission notification. Lazy looks at the icon for the notification. It's Cathode's TV icon.

"What's that app?"

"I programmed a signal sniffer to catch any time the code that the Eternal Light used to take over all of the display systems. It caught one."

"When... when did you have time to do that?"

Lazy stares slack-jawed at Cathode who ignores his stupid face and taps the icon opening a video feed on the dash. Solis is in a new location with the two remaining scientists standing, restrained arms behind their backs, off to the side of him. A man Cathode knows as a lab partner of Thibodeaux's named Malcolm, and her aunt. Solis is at the end of a religious rant.

"Like a thief in the night. The gog and the magog are among us. The Dajjal are here. But God sent no worms. The disease will not kill them. The second coming of the light will. It will awaken the Dabbat al-Ardd. It will ignite the seven suns into one eternal flame. The eternal light-"

Something unheard on the feed makes him pause.

"Oh, we have confirmed connection? Wonderful. You. Yes, you. I wish we did not have to meet this way. All this could have been completely avoided had they just given us what we wanted in the first place. So, now we are here. It can not be changed. We must make a deal. Work together. We require one thing of you and we need it now. We know you have the key to the future. We know you're receiving our message. We will meet at these coordinates, peacefully."

A set of numbers appear in a lower third on the screen. Cathode is already logging them as Solis continues.

"It will be exactly twelve fifteen mid-lunar hour. Bring us the key and we will let your relations go free."

Cathode freezes in place. Her Lunar GPS app loads awaiting the coordinates but she's glued to the dash screen.

"Oh no... they know Bridget is my aunt."

"If you fail to arrive at that specified time, or bring any thing that resembles protection, we will have to kill her. If you do not believe us serious... Well, that is a shame. I can feel it from you. You must have proof. Resolve. You must. It is needed. Yes? Yes. Needed."

Solis peers back and points at Malcolm, who looks at Solis in absolute fear. A gunshot clips the audio on the video feed, leaving it grotesquely silent as Malcolm's head snaps and he falls out of frame. Bridget begins screaming but the sound is still muted. It comes back as she repeats herself.

"DON'T BRING IT! DON'T COME BACK FOR ME! DON'T!"

Solis waves his hand at someone off frame.

"Leave him. Take her to the ship, please."

Bridget fights as two cultists lift her with ease and carry her off as she continues to scream.

"PLEASE! DON'T!"

Cathode's expression is ice. She slowly grits her teeth behind closed lips. Lazy sits shocked. Solis leisurely cranes his head toward the camera. A twisted Cheshire smile stretches across his face. Through his smiling teeth he speaks.

"Go in peace in the eternal light."

The feed ends. Cathode is loading in the coordinates from her personal GPS app into the ship's navigation system. Lazy softly chews on his lower lip.

"That's a trap, right? Like, we don't have any other options. We've got to save Bridget. Even if we go to the LF we already know they have people on the inside. So, they'd let him know. Trap, right? We have to go. But, what do we have for assurance? The promise of a crazy cultist guy? The promise of a crazy cultist guy. Yeah."

"Lazy."

Cathode hangs her head for a moment. She slowly turns, taking a deep breath and looks Lazy in the eyes. Her eyes ringed red.

"Stop. Please."

Lazy opens his mouth to respond but catches himself and just nods his head slightly. Cathode exhales heavily. A small smirk forms on her face.

"We have something for assurance."

Lazy's brow frumples as he looks down at his empty hands. Cathode points in a sweeping arc at the interior of the ship.

"We can teleport."

His head pointed straight up at the ceiling, Lazy's mouth goes slack. His cheeks tighten into a large smile.

"Yes, we can."

Lazy sits himself up straight as they both reset the ring systems. Cathode taps the navigation system, saves the meeting point pin for later and brings up a solar system map zoomed into the three planets they're nearest too. She starts searching for something. Lazy finishes his reset and looks at the solar map.

"What are you looking for?"

"We should leave the rings somewhere they aren't going to shift too much. We just did a quick shot with very little time for gravitational distortion of coordinates."

"Yeah, I was just about to say that about the distortions too, but go on."

Cathode clenches her fist at Lazy who smiles, confident in his joking comment.

"Right, so, we want to put it where celestial pull will make it remain almost still. We should put it here."

Cathode twists the map to show a space between the orbital paths of Venus and Earth. Almost dead center between the two paths. Lazy nods and rubs the chin area of his visor.

"Can we make it there and back to Luna in time?"

"It took all of thirty minutes to get to where we are. Why wouldn't we?"

"This is just some random spot in space we stopped at. We need to slow down and land on a moving, very solid rock."

Cathode quickly checks her clock.

"We've got over an hour."

Lazy slides his hands over the top of his helmet to his back.

"If you think we can do it safely."

Cathode sets the navigation system to adjust their angle and move forward.

"Unless you've got another plan. We give them the key fob, get my aunt back and use the rings if we need to get out of there fast."

"If they have the key fob, they can arm the bomb. They can lock us out of the ship."

Lazy picks up the key fob from the center console pouch and examines it as Cathode sets the throttle. The Superfluous slows down as they near the point in space she picked.

"If we don't leave the ship we won't get locked out. It's just ornamental after that. We don't need it to restart the ship. They can't kill its power from the key fob."

Tapping a soft plastic pack on his forearm Lazy opens his wrist tool kit, filled with tools usable while wearing spacesuit gloves. He carefully removes a small flat head screwdriver with his right hand. Pinching the key fob between his left thumb and forefinger, he guides the screwdriver into a small gap on the middle of the key fob. Gently, he twists the screwdriver popping apart the key fob's two clamshell sides. The top floats away. Lazy grabs it and sticks it to the adhesive pad in his forearm tool kit. Applying pressure to make sure it's stuck and he returns his attention to the key fob bottom that holds the device's electronic guts. With a quick twist of the screwdriver he dislodges the coin battery from the key fob. He catches it after it bounces off the ceiling of the cabin. Sticking it to the adhesive pad, Lazy then pulls the key fob top off. With a little click the clam shell snaps back together. He holds it up in front of Cathode.

"Won't stop them for long but definitely will be a pain in the butt trying to find a replacement battery."

"That's... actually really clever. Nice."

"I know. It doesn't happen often."

Cathode engages the exit ring release system. It whines with a low grinding noise and the ring's thrusters take it out to the exact point Cathode picked. She looks at the key fob.

"And if he tests it and it doesn't work?"

"We show him the battery and he can have it when we're all on the ship and can leave safely."

Cathode takes the key fob from Lazy and places it in her suit's wrist tool kit. Lazy delicately hands her the battery which she places in the corner of her adhesive pad to hide it from view. Flicking the flight stick, Cathode spins the Superfluous around back toward Luna. She considers it for a moment and then nods at Lazy's hand.

"That is a good enough plan."

"I'll take 'good enough'."

Cathode reloads the meeting point pin and activates it in the navigation system. She lays her hand on the throttle.

"What a day."

"And it's not over yet."

"You're the worst co-pilot. I need you to know that before the day actually ends."

"Affirmative, Captain."

Pushing the throttle, the Superfluous begins accelerating again. Cathode taps through the navigation system and sets the auto lander system to take care of the rest of the trip. The ship lurches as the system takes over controls, making micro adjustments to the angle of acceleration to approach Luna. Cathode glances at

Lazy before tapping her helmet's communications. She mutes their channel and opens a voice recorder app. She stares off into the dark infinity of space for a moment. She licks her lips and sets the app to record.

"Mom. First, I... I'm fine. I don't know what's going to happen but don't go home in case of... in case. I- Just take Mikko somewhere safe. I don't know if the city is still locked down or- I just need you to go somewhere not home to be safe and I will come find you after I rescue Aunt Bridget."

She stops the recording.

That sounds so stupid. This IS so stupid.

Sighing her finger floats between "Send" and "Delete". She nearly flicks "Delete" but selects "Send" instead. She chooses her mother's contact and taps her helmet to open up the communication channel again. Lazy is awkwardly singing loudly to himself.

"What are you doing?"

"I- I just didn't want to, um, interrupt."

"What?"

Lazy parts his lips in a toothy grimace.

"Your comms channel only muted incoming signals."

Cathode's face feels hot. She knows it's turning red. Her head curls forward as she squints her eyes. Slowly, she rotates to look at Lazy.

"It sounded stupid right?"

"Nah. It sounded good. Confident. We'll get her."

"Did you want to send your dad a message or something?"

Lazy breaks eye contact with Cathode and looks out the front of the ship as Luna appears in front of them, growing rapidly. He looks down and away. Thinking.

"No."

Cathode just nods. The Superfluous begins to rumble as it slows down. Their view twists as the ship changes its angle to curve around the moon, still slowing down. The point chosen by Solis is a barren stretch of rock at the edge of the dark side of the moon. The Superfluous' navigation system pings and the ship appears to stop completely before lowering straight down. Lazy checks the landing camera on the bottom of the ship and sees three ships already waiting. Two cult skiffs and a larger shiny luxury transport christened "The Aeos" according to the fancy calligraphy on its hull. Cathode taps the navigation menu again and sets the landing configuration so the Superfluous lands showing the other ships its backside. Lazy takes a few quick breaths.

"Good. good. All according to plan. Show them our ass. Dominate the-"

"Stop."

The ship lands, kicking out a soft gray cloud of dust around its landing thrusters. Cathode unlocks her seatbelt and pushes off to the cargo hold. Lazy taps the pilot controls system to shift control over to his seat. He loads every available camera he can onto the dash display. He watches as Cathode lowers herself down and gives a thumbs up when she's at the back of the cargo hold. Lazy taps the hatch release and the cargo hold door unlocks, beginning to open. Cathode grips the key fob in her hand. She looks at her open wrist tool kit, sees the battery in the corner of the adhesive pad and then snaps it shut. The door shudder clanks as it fully opens. Cathode carefully steps out to the edge. She hesitates. She scans the ships ahead of her. The skiff pilots both sit in their cockpits looking right back at her.

Solis walks out in a gold toned space suit with a ridiculous starburst shaped helmet. He smiles that empty smile as he pulls Bridget forward. She's in an ill fitting spacesuit and her arms are zip tied behind her back. She struggles to get away but Solis is strong enough to drag her along. Cathode takes a single step down to the lunar surface. She can feel the rocks shifting under her feet. She can hear her own heartbeat in her ears. She holds up her fist. She opens it to reveal the key fob. Solis and Bridget stop about a yard away from the Superfluous. Solis throws Bridget down. She lands hard on her shoulder but immediately tries to scramble away. Solis steps on her ankle stopping her. He raises his hand and beckons Cathode to come out to him. She takes a quick look into the back camera and nods to Lazy ever so slightly. Cathode taps her helmet, opening up her communication settings. She selects "open public channel" and speaks directly to Solis as she stomps forward with as much confidence as she can muster.

"Let her up. I'll give you the key. Only after she's safely on the ship."

The smile on Solis' face doesn't wane. He speaks again through his sharp white teeth.

"Splendid."

Twisting his foot before he lifts it, Solis lets Bridget get up to a seated position. Shaking her head she's trying to yell at Cathode but her helmet communications are off. She continues to shake her head as she gets to her feet. Cathode stops and backs up as her aunt tries to run away from them. Solis lifts a remote from his wrist and taps a large button on its top. Bridget shakes violently and falls over. She twitches slightly. Cathode takes a step back toward the ship.

"What did you do to her?!"

"Nothing to worry about. It is merely a low level shock collar. For control. She will be totally fine."

Solis raises his hand and makes a waving motion toward Bridget. A large cultist appears from the back of the luxury cruiser, unarmed Cathode notes. The large cultist walks over to Bridget and picks her up easily. Cathode takes another step back as both the large cultist and Solis advance on her. Gently placing Bridget in the cargo hold on the door hinges the large cultist stands on the edge of the Superfluous. Cathode feels him looking at her as Solis steps up to her. He holds his palm out to her, still smiling.

"Now, if you would so please."

Cathode looks at the large cultist again. Solis waves him away. With no regard for the situation the large cultist lumbers back toward the luxury cruiser. Solis lifts his open hand again. Cathode gets one foot on the cargo hatch and drops the key fob into his hand. She leaps back into the ship and grips onto the ceiling grip bar. Solis doesn't move. He turns the key fob over in his hand examining it. Cathode pounds her fist against the interior wall.

"Go Lazy!"

The Superfluous kicks up a new wave of lunar dust as the thrusters engage. The dust swirls around Solis who looks up at them as the ship takes off moving up and forward. Cathode uses a small wire cutter to snip off the zip ties on

Bridget's wrists and taps her helmet. Bridget is groggy from the shock but she quickly collects herself. She pushes Cathode back.

"No! No, let me off!"

"Bridget! It's ok. We took the battery out. We-"

The ship hums as the entrance ring begins to move. Lazy has activated the ring system.

"You don't understand!"

Cathode can't hold Bridget down. Twisting her weight Bridget forcefully throws Cathode toward the front of the ship.

"He put a bomb in my suit!"

"What?!"

Cathode looks past her aunt to see Solis standing in the settling dust. He wiggles his fingers at them in a perverse wave before tapping the second button on his shock collar remote. The ring system activates and the Superfluous begins to go through the entrance ring's wormhole. A dull red light flashes from inside the chest of Bridget's suit.

"You activated the rings? Oh no! NO!"

Cathode watches in horror as Bridget leaps from the Superfluous' open hatch back toward the lunar surface. The Superfluous passes completely through the exit ring. Cathode sees a fire rise from her aunt's chest just as the entrance ring passes through the exit ring and the system deactivates. The wormhole closes like a water droplet. The hatch doors begin shutting as Cathode screams.

She screams at the stars.

Lazy lowers himself down into the cargo hold where Cathode is floating in the fetal position. Her tears have pooled around her eyes. Lazy watches her for a moment. Unsure what to do or say.

Go away. Everything. Just go away.

Cathode straightens out and grabs a wall rung. She pulls herself into the wall hard. Hard enough to force the tears off her eyes. The two warbling spheres of water bounce off her visor and scatter around the interior of her helmet. She blinks a few times. Lazy leans over to see her face but she's staring into the wall.

"Hey... Are you okay? I mean, I know you're not."

Cathode continues to stare blankly.

"No, I'm not. I don't know what he's planning but we're stopping him. I don't care how."

Lazy tries to smirk big enough that Cathode sees it.

"I figured that was part of the plan the whole time."

She looks at him and tries to smile weakly. Suddenly, she kicks off and grabs Lazy in a bear hug knocking him back. He catches a wall rung and holds on.

Cathode doesn't let go. Lazy lays his free arm on her back and gently hugs back for a moment.

"Hey, we teleported. Again."

Cathode lets out a weak whimper of a laugh.

"Yes. We did. Again."

She grips onto the wall rung, pulls away from Lazy and swings her body up to the cockpit door.

Just keep moving. Don't think about it. Just keep going. Don't. Don't. No thinking. Only action. Action!

Cathode sits back in the pilot seat of the Superfluous. She checks the oxygen settings. Lazy sits down in the co-pilot seat. Cathode verifies the hatch to the cargo hold is fully sealed. She sets the atmospheric controls for the cockpit. Hissing oxygen begins to seep in from several small vents. A list of gasses and ratios display on the dash. The list goes from red to orange to green. Cautiously Cathode clicks open the neck release of her helmet. With a tiny metal ping she twists it off and lifts it over her head. She latches it to a strap in the ceiling. She takes a deep breath. Holds it. Looks to Lazy. And releases.

"All good. Bit of an odor to it but better than my suit right now."

Lazy has his helmet off and is latching it to his own strap as Cathode begins to charge the ring system again. Lazy runs a hand through his sweaty hair.

"So, if I'm guessing correctly, we're resetting the ring system. Because that works. Like, awesome. Amazing. Super thermal. And then we... um, what?"

Cathode slides off her suit glove, runs her somewhat pruney hand through her own hair and rests her goggles on the top of her head. She taps through a few random menus, thinking. She rubs her red swollen eyes softly.

"They have the bomb, the lock, no battery and supposedly limited time. What does that say to you?"

Lazy clips his gloves to his helmet and rubs his hands together.

"They need to get a battery fast, set the bomb and, uh, use it?"

Cathode nods and resets her goggles over her eyes.

"Use it how though?"

"It's on the moon. So, blow up the whole moon? Can they do that? Can it do that?"

"I didn't work on it. I don't know. I mean I do. I guess."

"You guess?"

"If it's built on the same power system as this ship it's supposedly exponentially infinite. Or at least until the containment system can't hold it anymore. I don't even remotely know where to begin to calculate that ratio though. Even Bridget-"

Cathode nearly chokes on her name.

"Bridget had to have an entire server array do those type of calculations. But, the moon is definitely possible."

"Possible? Earth?"

Cathode tilts her head to the side, pokes her tongue into her left inner cheek for a moment. She squints her eyes, shifting her tongue to the other side. Her eyes slowly open wider and she angles her view toward the light source right in front of them. She holds her hand up to it.

"The sun."

"I'm sorry. What?"

"Solis. Helios. Sun god. They're going to shoot it into the sun. An exponential energy loop bomb powered by an entire star..."

Lazy stares at the sun through his goggles' UV filters, which are set to max.

"I- I don't want to say it."

"If it even gets close it'll wipe out at least half the galaxy. Easily."

"Yes, I didn't want to say that."

They both stare for a moment longer at the sun. Cathode clicks her tongue.

"They need a clean shot. The timing is for when the path is clearest. They'll also need a point to launch it from."

Cathode waves her hand in front of her goggles and brings up Margaret's contact. She taps it. Margaret immediately picks up.

"Wo de tian na! Catherine, are you okay?!"

"What? Hold on, I'm patching you into the deck."

Cathode flips her wrist and sends the call to the Superfluous' audio system. Margaret keeps talking.

"We saw the news drone footage! Is Bradley okay?! That explosion!"

Lazy speaks first.

"Hey, Marge. We're both... not fine, but alive. How are you?"

"Bradley? Oh. Oh, that's good. I'm good. We're safe. Like I just said my mom and I saw the live news feed drone footage. We saw the ships and the cultists, and... the other stuff."

"Yeah, there has been a lot going on here. Listen, we-"

"Who was the person?

The question echoes around the cockpit. Margaret, not receiving a response, clarifies it.

"The one that fell out of the ship. The news drone- I guess somebody saw your ship making its landing descent, and the camera drone was flying toward you but it was still kind of far out when... when it happened."

Lazy leans in his chair and stares at the floor. Cathode lets her head drift back to look up at the ceiling. She can feel her eyes watering again. She blinks.

"It was my aunt- Aunt Bridget. She knew the cultists put an explosive on her before we made the trade off. She jumped out to save us."

"I'm so sor-"

"Listen, we gave them the key fob. It's what can activate the bomb. There was a bomb inside the ship. We accidentally dropped that on our initial escape from the lab."

"They have a bomb now?!"

"Calm down. Actually, don't. But, still listen. They're going to shoot it at the sun in an attempt to wipe out the galaxy. At least that's what we've figured."

There is a long audible sigh on Margaret's end followed by low mumbling.

"You need me to calculate where they're launching the bomb from. I've already started."

Cathode lets a small smile break across her lips. Lazy smiles wide, nodding and staring straight ahead. With a heavy exhale Cathode grips onto her arm rests and sits herself up straight in her chair.

"I knew we had to call you. Once you have that send it to us. After that send it to both the news, so there are eyes on it, and the Lunar Frontiersmen. But they've infiltrated the LF. So, try to do a mass dump on an extranet email chain for the local base."

"Noted."

Cathode glances at Lazy.

"Anything else?"

"No, I think that covers it. I think we should be calling it a missile instead of a bomb but... yes. Covered."

Margaret hums for a moment.

"Uuuuum. I am sorry about your aunt, Catherine. Really. But, can I just say one thing."

Cathode is still looking at Lazy who shrugs back at her.

"Yeah, sure."

"This is SUPER exciting! You guys are on like a super top secret spy mission! It's dangerous and wild and- Sorry, sorry. It's just a lot of information coming at me real quick so I need to get one out."

"One what?"

"WO CAO!"

Lazy immediately buckles over trying not to laugh but can't stop, even with his jaw clenched. Cathode shakes her head and lets out a nasally chuckle. Lazy leans into the center console even though he doesn't need to for Manticore to hear him.

"This is insane right, Margaret?"

"If it was anyone else I'd say yes. I still think yes, but only a little. I know who I'm talking to."

Cathode nods in agreement which makes Lazy force down a laugh again.

"Got it."

Cathode pauses for a beat, confused.

"Got what?"

"The area they'll have to launch from within the next hour that would result in a clear direct path to the sun. Within a range of, uh, about twenty miles. I'm sending you the coordinates and the flight path."

Cathode sees an incoming file notification. She accepts it. The download starts. Their distance from the extranet's nearest relay satellite makes the speed slower.

"This is pretty soon. When is the next window Luna is within a clear view of the sun?"

"One month. Give or take a few days. I'm not sure of the course altering abilities of the bomb. Sorry, missile."

"The speed at which it can travel, if this ship is any indication, it wouldn't be able to course correct at all at a top speed. And it can get to that speed quick."

The download completes and Cathode throws it to the dash display. She and Lazy look at the flight path. They aren't too far off from where it passes between Mercury and Venus. Lazy starts working on the distance and timing they would need to intercept based on the speed he'd experienced the Superfluous doing earlier.

"If we leave the exit ring where it is now we'd need to hit it going about one twentieth the speed of light, minimum, when the bomb is here."

He taps a point close to the Venus orbital path. He taps it again to leave a digital mark on the flight path map. Margaret chirps up over the audio system.

"What's the exit ring?"

Cathode furrows her brow momentarily.

"It's the exit ring for the ship's teleportation system."

There is silence. Lazy looks to the dash to see the call is still connected.

"Marge?"

A low hiss rises over the speakers.

"Yoooooooou TELEPORT!? WHAT?! WHAT?! WHAT?! WHAT?!"

Cathode puts her face in her palms. Lazy's laughter comes out in sputters. He nods at Cathode.

"Uh, yeah Marge. This ship teleports. It uses a dual ring system to create a worm-"

"A wrinkle in time."

"-hole. Wait, what?"

"Like folding a paper over two matching punch holes. The punch holes are the rings. Yeah? Right?"

Cathode covers her mouth and then wipes her lips.

"I should have brought you along instead of Lazy."

"Hey!"

A crackly ping echoes out of the speakers. Margaret sniffs.

"Hmm. Those launch coordinates have been sent to the two closest News stations and the LF base email chain. Anything else?"

Lazy shakes his head at Cathode. She leans forward to end the call.

"No, I don't think so, Manticore."

"Good. Your order is ready. Please pull forward to the pick-up window."

Lazy slaps his arm rest.

"Ha! Good one."

Cathode lets herself smile again.

"Thanks. Stay safe. This will be over soon."

"You guys come back safe too so we can, like, teleport to Mars or something."

"Yeah... bye."

Cathode ends the call before Margaret can respond. She closes her eyes and lets her arms float in the zero gravity. Lazy scratches the back of his head.

"She's a weird one, huh? So, now we go stop the bad guy?"

Cathode raises her arms to the ceiling.

"I want to say- I want to go home. I want to say we go home and everything will work itself out. But-"

"But, we know the LF can't be trusted and the News won't intervene. AND have no idea how dangerous the situation is."

"Correct."

"And our chance of survival remains low."

"Also correct."

Lazy raises his left hand toward Cathode and makes a fist. He nods at her. She makes a fist and bumps his. He dramatically explodes his hand away. She weakly mirrors him.

"Let's go fuck up Solis' day."

Cathode grips the flight stick of the Superfluous.

"Yes. Let's."

The ship spins off its adjustment thrusters and Cathode punches the throttle forward.

The Superfluous begins to slow as it approaches Margaret's theorized Eternal Light cult launch area. As the ship rattles to a cruising speed Lazy immediately flips on high magnification on the ship cameras and his goggles. He also sets one eye to a thermographic view setting. Cathode's signal sniffing app chimes again.

"He's broadcasting again. We're close."

Cathode opens a video window. A handheld camera is aimed at Solis, in his bizarre space suit, as he marches back and forth in front of a derelict lunar satellite and asteroid defense launch pad that has been retrofitted to launch the bomb. He's almost leaping as he shouts.

"... and we, the chosen of the light. The cleansers. The cleaners. We stand here today ready to return Phaethon to his father."

Cathode notices that the cult has scrawled "PHAETHON" onto the side of the bomb in vibrant golden paint.

"See them yet? The launch pad looks like it is kind of short."

Solis continues his speech on the video screen.

"He has given us such joy, power, warmth. And we must offer this mere tribute in hopes to cleanse this universe of the coming darkness. We mere mortals will be the torchbearers to get it done. Yes, we will. You, and you and you."

Solis points to cultists in the small crowd in front of the camera. He points into the camera.

"And even you. You may not know it but you have all helped us reach this pinnacle. The tip of the arrow head. A beautiful dory of energy. What I do here today I do for everything. There will be no Fimbulvetr. No great winter. Let us pray. We invoke You, the Greatest God, Eternal Lord, World Ruler, who are over the World and under the World. Inside all of us, shining from the center for the whole galaxy. Never setting. Speak to us. Benevolent Lord makes us your lucky Agathos Daimons. We call upon Your Holy and Great and Hidden Names which You rejoice to hear. The galaxy flourished when You shone forth, and Gaia became fruitful when you laughed; us animals begat our young when You permitted. Give glory and honor and favor and fortune and power to this oblation we consecrate today for You."

Solis stomps around the launch pad as he ramps up the intensity of his prayer.

"We invoke You, the greatest in Heaven, the Shining Helios, giving Light throughout the universe. You are the Great Serpent, Leader of all the Gods, who has controlled since before the beginnings of Kemet and the End of the Whole Inhabited World, who mate in the ocean. You are He who becomes visible each day and sets in the Northwest of Heaven, and rises in the Southeast. Our deathless God. Pierce us with your golden gaze. Hail to you Lord! Hail! Hail Helios!"

Lazy continues to scan across a large, relatively normal, field of minor craters when he catches a heat signature past a rim off to his right. He triggers the ship cameras to follow his goggle view and zoom in with better magnification. Solis finishes his rant with his arms punched toward the sun. The cultists standing around outside their skiffs raise their fists in the air. They all point with their whole hands to the sun. Frozen in their salute as Solis walks to the bomb. Cathode sees a News camera drone flying toward the crater off to her left. She taps Lazy's shoulder and points it out. He motions off to the right as a single LF fighter hooks over the curvature of the lunar surface and races toward the same launch pad crater.

"I know I was all gung ho about this. But, it looks like Marge's message got through. So, maybe we just sit back?"

Cathode throttles up.

"No. We stop them. Whatever it takes."

Lazy tightens his lips flat on his face and nods vigorously. He cinches his seatbelt tighter.

"Right. You're right. Let's crash this party."

"Literally."

Cathode twists the flight stick and aims the Superfluous directly at the small launch pad. Lazy grabs his helmet and gloves. He puts the gloves on, clicks the helmet into place and grips onto his chair. Cathode does the same. More fighters appear, off in the distance, behind the initial LF ship. The cultists' skiffs parked around the launch pad spring to life, lifting off and turning to intercept the fighters. Cathode looks at the first fighter ship.

"He's going too fast."

The fighter's pilot seems to be aware of this. The LF fighter curves toward the Superfluous' path just as the quickest cultist skiff to lift off fires at it. Lazy watches as the fighter does an extremely quick drop in speed and course correction.

"He was just the scout. They thought it might have been a fake message. He was sent to check and only called the rest when he saw the launch pad. They're going to be too late."

The fighter crosses directly in front of the Superfluous causing Cathode to pull up and over as the pursuing skiff continues after the LF scout fighter. Cathode grits her teeth as she corrects her course and sees Solis.

"We are too."

Lazy looks out in disbelief as the bomb, with Solis riding it like a psychotic rodeo bull rider, takes off and immediately begins to accelerate. Cathode twists the stick and dodges two skiffs dog fighting with the arriving LF fighters. She hooks through a second group firing at each other. No one is chasing the bomb besides them. She pulls back on the stick and slams the throttle forward. Lazy looks momentarily sick, shoved back into his chair, as the Superfluous fires straight off the lunar surface at an incredible rate. Cathode leans into the g-force. Even at one sixth the g-force of Earth the pull of the moon is enough to nearly knock them both out. Lazy pulls himself forward and checks Margaret's flight path. He tags the bomb and overlays it on top of the chart. It's an almost one to one match. He checks the ship speed and adds their path to the chart. They can see the bomb in front of them. It's barely a speck at normal magnification but it's there. Lazy taps the dash to bring up one of the ship's front cameras in a window. He magnifies it to see Solis riding the bomb.

They pass the Earth's orbital path. Casually, Solis looks back. He stands up, his magne-boots keeping him locked to the bomb's surface, and turns to face them. Cathode watches him intently.

"We're not going to catch it. Call it when we need to use the rings."

Lazy sets a countdown timer. He has placed a red dot on the flight path that is causing the countdown.

"When that hits we go. What is he doing?"

Solis puts his arms out like he's looking for a hug. Cathode can't really see it but she knows he's got that creepy smile smeared over his face.

The only thing that'll be left of you will be those teeth orbiting Venus.

Solis lifts his palms as if he heard Cathode's thoughts. He reaches down and grips his magne-boots. Lazy looks up from the count down timer.

"Wha-"

With a tap of his fingers Solis releases his boots from the bomb and with the softest of taps he kicks off. He grows in the magnified camera view. Cathode can now make out his smile. Lazy's eyes grow as if they're trying to escape his face.

"He's going to hit us?!"

The count down timer chimes. Cathode clicks the rings' system activation. The entrance ring begins to shift forward.

"He'll be floating, dead in space. We'll get ahead of the bomb, disarm it and be done with all this."

Lazy keeps watching as Solis drifts closer. The entrance ring reaches the front of the ship. Cathode taps the "activate". She mimics Solis' smile.

Nothing happens.

A warning sign flashes on the dash "Ring Error". Cathode's smile disappears.

"What? What is happening?!"

She tries to reactivate it but the system just chimes back at her and repeats the error. Cathode looks up to see Solis closing the distance.

"I can't dodge him. We won't be able to reach the bomb if we change course."

Lazy tries to dig through the menus. He opens a crash report file.

"We can't reach it anyway. We need to get ahead of it. We're both moving at the same speed now. The ring is already in use... What? That's impossible. I don't-"

Cathode pulls up the same crash report file. She sees the exit ring no longer registers as active. As if it just vanished. Lazy quickly tries to reboot the exit ring but gets no response. Cathode watches in terror as Solis grows in the front view screen.

With a soft thud, and a louder metal to metal grinding click of his boots, Solis lands on the Superfluous. He confidently walks in front of the cockpit. He leans forward with eyes impossibly wide and that grotesque smile. He holds up the key fob and clicks it. Lazy taps the close hatch button. Another error code pops up; "Door Controlled Remotely". He unbuckles himself and turns over his chair toward the cargo hold.

"Keep trying to fix the rings. I'll- I'll stop him."

Solis struts over the top of the cockpit toward the cargo hold's doors that are still opening. Lazy pulls the cockpit door open and rides the venting oxygen out. He activates his own boots when he reaches the cargo hold floor. Solis steps over the upper lip of the top cargo hold door. He stands looking at an upside down Lazy. Lazy taps his wrist tool kit and pulls out his screwdriver. Solis reaches to the sun crest on the chest of his spacesuit and slides a menacing tactical knife out from behind it. His smile never shifts. Lazy waves his free hand at Solis in a "come on" motion. Solis takes off in a clunky magnetic sprint curving from the ceiling, to the wall as Lazy charges him in an opposing path. Solis, now at a horizontal angle to Lazy, stabs his knife upward. Lazy shifts to his left foot and spins on his toes to avoid the stab. As he spins he sees Cathode diving from the cockpit ladder at Solis. She has her own screwdriver in her hand. Solis clicks his heels to deactivate his magne-boots and kicks off the wall to avoid Cathode. Cathode lashes out as they pass each other and scrapes her screwdriver across his right boot. Her screwdriver shears off his boots power cords sending sparks flying. Solis uses the twisting momentum from Cathode's attack and sticks his left foot to the ceiling. Lazy runs up the wall, disengages his boots and swings at Solis' chest. Leaning back Solis easily dodges the swing and kicks Lazy with his left foot, sending Lazy bouncing off the floor. Cathode catches herself before falling out the back hatch and re-engages her boots. Lazy and Cathode stand on the floor on opposite sides of Solis. He looks from Cathode to Lazy and spins his knife in front of his chest in zero gravity. The bi-stable state makes the knife flip from aiming at Lazy to aiming at Cathode as it spins. Cathode looks past him at Lazy.

"Disable his other boot."

Lazy nods at Cathode. He reaches out, grabbing a safety harness strap off the wall and throws it at Solis with a snap. The snap causes it to spin and expand open as it flies at Solis. Lazy kicks off after it. Solis turns his head to see Lazy but keeps his body at profile between the two. Cathode flips to the ceiling, locks her boots. She lines up, disengages her boots and charges at Solis. As the strap reaches Solis he snatches his knife from the air with his right hand and deftly slices the strap in two. With his left hand he grabs one of the pieces and whip cracks it toward Cathode. Cathode is forced to catch the end buckle before it snaps into her helmet's visor. Disengaging his boot, Solis pushes off to the floor and pulls the strap back at Lazy. Cathode is yanked into Lazy with additional force. Lazy lets go of his screwdriver, reaches out and catches Cathode before they smash into each other. He rotates her around his body as they meet, grabs the strap from her hand and lets her go, drifting to the front wall of the cargo hold. Solis yanks at the strap and pulls Lazy toward him. Lazy engages his boots but is too far from the ceiling to catch and is dragged right into Solis. Cathode catches a rung of the cockpit ladder and turns just as Lazy's left foot magnetizes to the floor and Solis shoves his knife deep into Lazy's stomach. Cathode screams.

"No!"

Lazy grips onto Solis' hand and keeps the knife stuck into his abdomen. Solis smiles at Lazy. Lazy smiles right back. The Cheshire smile finally fades from Solis' face. With both hands Lazy grips onto Solis' hands over the knife handle and lifts his right knee as if to kick Solis away. Solis pulls his left hand from Lazy's grip to block it but Lazy stops raising his knee just as Solis hand shifts. Lazy opens his lips in a mimicking toothy smile. Cathode rips the fire extinguisher off the wall next to the ladder. Just before he stomps his right foot down Cathode sees that Lazy had caught his screwdriver, perfectly vertical, with his magne-boot. The tip of the screwdriver goes straight down through Solis' left boot. Solis screams inside his helmet as blood and sparks fly out from under Lazy's boot. Lazy leans back, still gripping onto Solis' other hand and uses the forehead of his helmet to headbutt Solis' visor. The glass splinters as Solis' head snaps backward. Cathode rushes over, stomping up behind them.

"Duck right."

Lazy, maintaining his death grip like hold on Solis' arm, leans off to his right as Cathode swings her screwdriver directly into the cracked spiderwebbed glass of Solis' visor. The head of her screwdriver punctures the visor, pierces through Solis' upper lip, smashing out a swath of his front teeth and sending blood splattering across the interior of his visor. The screwdriver is lodged up to the handle, which stopped it from going deeper, in his visor. Air hisses out around the edge of the handle. As Cathode lets go of her screwdriver Lazy pushes Solis' right hand and knife out away from his stomach. He takes a large step away by sliding his right foot straight back, tearing the screwdriver across and out of Solis' mangled boot. This causes more blood and sparks to scatter across the cargo hold. Solis, screaming in his helmet, flails his knife around wildly. He's not able to see or magnetize to a surface anymore. Lazy grips his stomach tight, disengages his right boot and kicks the now free screwdriver at Solis. It bounces off his right shoulder causing Solis to spin his knife wildly off to his side. Cathode, approaching from his left, rams the fire extinguisher into Solis' stomach and yanks the pin. The fire extinguisher releases foam onto Cathode and launches Solis out the back of the Superfluous.

He quickly shrinks into the black void. A cartoonish plume of white foam trails him.

Cathode wipes most of the foam from her suit and turns to help Lazy back up into the cockpit. He lets her drag him up as he keeps pressure on his suit. Lazy looks out the open hatch at the stars.

"That was a thing."

"Yeah. Yeah, it was. Now we have to deal with the other thing."

"Right. Sun bomb."

Lazy eases away as they enter the cockpit and slowly pulls himself down into the co-pilot chair with his free hand. Cathode engages her boots as she lands in a seated position on the pilot chair and quickly checks the flight path.

"Even if they worked… we've passed the exit ring."

"By a lot. We're passing Mercury."

Looking through the front panel Cathode can still see the bomb ahead of them. A tiny black dot traveling toward a massive, ever growing ball of pure energy. She leans back in her chair and chews her lip. Lazy winces as he tries to adjust in his seat.

"Any possible way to catch up at this point?"

"If there is, it's not coming to me."

With a laugh Lazy winces again and coughs.

"I could get out and push. Would that help?"

Cathode smiles, closing her eyes. She can feel the tears pooling already. She strains to sound happy.

"Yes."

Lazy laughs harder and grits his teeth. Cathode can see blood seeping around his gums.

"I'll get right on that. Just going to need a fifteen minute break."

"No time."

"Oh, you're worse than Jeremy."

Cathode takes one last look at the bomb off in the distance and grabs the throttle. She looks at Lazy who nods. She pulls back on the throttle and the ship begins to slow. The bomb disappears into the brightness of the sun. Lazy checks the flight path as the bomb's tracking point gets further away from the Superfluous. He taps the screen and a countdown timer appears. It runs down from two minutes as the bomb's tracking point inches closer to the sun. Cathode holds out her right hand and makes a fist in anger. She stares at her fist until she has to blink out the tear pools around her eyes. Her face softens. She flexes her fist. Turning to Lazy she holds up her fist to him. He swaps his hands on his wound and lifts his left hand. He makes a fist and looks at the count down timer.

They both watch it hit zero. Lazy taps his fist into Cathodes and pulls it back. A string of blood pulls between the two as they wiggle their fingers in an explosion. The sun's brightness suddenly surges to the point that they both have to shield their eyes even with UV filters on max. The sun expands and grows toward them. Pure white energy rages at them. Cathode grabs for Lazy's floating left hand and grips it as the entirety of their existence turns pure white.

"Bye."

"Full popcorn."

The Superfluous fires out of the exit ring chased by a massive burst of white energy that causes both rings to explode behind the ship. Cathode blinks several times and opens her UV shield's irises. She looks around. Lazy sits with his eyes pinched shut. Cathode, still holding Lazy's hand, shakes it.

"We're alive."

Slowly, Lazy opens his eyes.

"Are you sure? This isn't some form of afterlife?"

An error message pops up on the ship's control panel, "You have left the predetermined flight path. Return? Y/N". Cathode taps "Y". Lazy stares in disbelief at the flight path.

"What. Is. Happening?!"

He traces a finger from their current position dot backward toward Luna. His finger glides over the bomb's dot and stops on a second Superfluous tracker. Cathode's jaw drops. Her eyes don't move as Lazy's hand drops away.

"We timed... this is... We time traveled...?"

"That's not possible. That's not a thing. It's not real. We're in purgatory on a loop or something. Sisyphus with a bomb instead of a boulder."

Cathode checks the flight path timing. She brings up a second panel showing their original flight path. She rewinds the recording of it back to the point that matches where the bomb and second Superfluous are currently.

"Play back with audio."

The rewound flight path recording begins playing with Cathode and Lazy talking to each other.

"What? What is happening?!"

The system chimes.

"I can't dodge him. We won't be able to reach the bomb if we change course."

"We can't reach it anyway. We need to get ahead of it. We're both moving at the same speed now. The ring is already in use... What? That's impossible. I don't-"

Cathode grips onto her chair.

"Pause playback. That's us right now. Not us us. But, them, us."

Cathode points back over her shoulder. Lazy's head whips back and forth from looking at Cathode's hand to the flight path panels. He grits his bloodied teeth.

"Right now?! We have to tell them to move!"

Cathode rapidly begins opening up audio controls. She quickly changes the connections protocol numbers and copies the original into her output. She test pings the new connection.

They both hold their breath.

The system returns a signal.

"Me! I mean Cathode! Change your course! Avoid Solis!"

"Who is this?!"

"Catherine! Just do it. We're ahead of you! We'll take care of the bomb!"

"You know about the- Fine!"

Lazy expands the current timeline flight path to take up as much space as possible on the dash screen. They watch as the second Superfluous icon swiftly curves away from the path and then begins a long curve back onto it. Lazy swaps hands over his stomach wound.

"Great. Bradley, my guy, you do not even know how good you got it right now."

There is a slight pause.

"Uh. You sound like me."

"I am you. And sitting next to me is also a Cathode. I know-"

Both Lazys speak at the same time.

"Brain-splosion. Plooie..."

Cathode stares at Lazy as he opens his free hand out and away from the top of his helmet. She turns back to her controls and begins to work on an acceleration equation.

"Cathode, ignore him. Them."

"Always do."

"I'm going to work out the deceleration and rapid re-acceleration I need to do so we can catch the bomb in the cargo hold. I'm going to have my Lazy send you all of the data of what happened to us. All of it. Whatever happened when the bomb hit the sun and the power surge to the ring system."

"Uh... roger? Copy that."

Cathode taps down the throttle and sets her new speed program to run. Their Superfluous' flight path tracker begins to slow as the bomb and second ship get closer.

"And stay within that distance of us until the transfer is complete to guarantee it's received. When..."

Lazy locks eyes with Cathode. He blinks and looks to the cargo hold.

"When it's time you curve out and away. I'm initiating that transfer now."

Lazy taps to select all of the system memory stores folders and sends a transmission request to the other Superfluous. They accept and the file begins transferring.

0%

Cathode waits to be sure that the status has moved.

1%

She returns to watch her speed program click faster incrementally. The bomb on the flight path inches closer.

2%

Lazy carefully lifts himself over his chair and floats toward the cargo hold. Cathode mutes comms to the other ship.

"Wait. I'll do it. You don't have to."

Lazy catches onto the cockpits's manual hand wheel and looks over Cathode's shoulder at the speed program clicking the acceleration higher as the tiny dot that is the bomb begins to take shape in the rear camera video screen.

"I trust your program. We can both do it."

Cathode floats over to Lazy and reaches past him to open the cockpit door. Lazy lays flat against the wall and watches the bomb grow even larger in the rear view camera as the ship nears terminal velocity.

8%

"Plus, I don't know if either of us will know what to do anyway. Might need an extra set of hands to slap it around."

Cathode passes through the open door and curls out flat against the wall as Lazy passes. She closes the cockpit door behind her.

"The extra hand is more than appreciated. I think it's going to take more than slaps though."

Cathode brings a copy of the data transfer progress bar up in her goggles.

10%

They enter the open backed cargo hold just as the bomb is within five meters. Cathode and Lazy watch as it seems to slowly float into the cargo hold. It inches forward until it's about to hit the cargo bay's front wall. Lazy reaches out but it slowly puts a tiny dent into the wall. Lazy clenches his teeth and leans back.

"It's not armed. That's why we're back here, remember?"

Lazy relaxes his body and swaps hands on his stomach.

"Obviously I did not."

Cathode begins to search the frame of the bomb on the right side while Lazy searches on the left. Cathode notices a raised panel under the T in PHAETHON. She reaches for her screwdriver. Her wrist tool box is empty. She didn't pull it out of Solis' faceplate.

"Lazy! Panel over here. I don't have my screwdriver. Come here."

Lazy floats over the top of the bomb and taps his foot on the ceiling to twist down to Cathode's side. He engages his boots and checks the panel.

"Mine's gone too."

He turns and walks around the cargo hold. He pauses at the holding arm for the, now gone, fire extinguisher. He taps the side of a black rectangular box next to the arm. A small door opens and Lazy reaches inside.

"We had an ax this whole time?!"

Lazy spins around with the small hand ax raised in his clenched fist.

"Come on! Jees."

44%

Cathode sees him coming with the ax and transfers to the other side, bracing up against the opposing side of the bomb. Lazy takes a swing with the ax and wedges it in between the panel and the bomb frame. He twists and the panel flies off bouncing around the cargo hold until Cathode swats it out into open space. She glides over the bomb to see what the exposed control panel looks like. Lazy holds the ax limp at his side. There isn't a control panel. Just a single charging port. Lazy backs up and brings the ax back like a baseball bat.

"You son of a-"

"Wait!"

Lazy stops mid-swing and wobbles as his magne-boots stop his momentum. Cathode walks over to a control panel on the wall of the cargo bay.

"That won't do anything. It needs to be primed. It needs energy. It's been using too much for propulsion."

53%

Cathode opens an inlaid container underneath the control panel. A spooled charge cable is inside. She unspools a few feet and walks back to the bomb pulling more as she goes.

"We just feed it ours until it's ready to burst and then dump the rest of ours to diminish any chance of an equally powerful energy loop explosion from the ship itself."

"And if that doesn't work I hit it a lot with the ax. Deal?"

Cathode plugs the charging cable into the bomb.

"Deal."

65%

Lazy walks around to the front of the bomb as it charges. He takes a few one handed practice swings. Cathode notices him swaying after he stops swinging. He lets go of the ax momentarily to adjust his hands. Cathodes passes him toward the cockpit.

77%

"I'm going to go verify the transfer is completed."

"Leaving me all alone?"

"I left the outbound comms on the ship muted."

"Right. Okay. So, how will I know this thing worked?"

Cathode transfers to the cockpit.

"You'll know if it works."

She sits in her chair and removes the data transfer status bar from her goggles as she can see it on the dash as well. She unmutes the comms channels.

Lazy's face has completely drained of color. Sweat sticks to his hair and face inside his helmet. His eyes go heavy and he fights to keep them open. The front tip of the bomb pops forward by an inch exposing a glowing core of energy. The light floods the entire cargo hold. Lazy lets go of the ax and turns his UV filter back on. He lets the ax float out of his weakened grip.

"Yeah, I'll know. I know. I-"

Lazy looks at the bomb for one last moment before climbing toward the cockpit.

"I knew it'd work."

89%

She feels like the data transmission percentage is moving at a horrible crawling rate. Looking up from the control panel all she can see through the front display is the burning white of the sun. Even filtered down to barely a hundredth of it's true strength it makes her eyes hurt. Off to the left she sees Venus. But, not her Venus. Using her gloved hand to shield her helmet face mask she looks back down to the control panel.

97%

Her hand floats over a throttle control. Even with her helmet on, the sound of the air leaking out of his suit catches her off guard. Lazy straps himself down in his seat. He gives a weak thumbs up with his left hand. Looking past his left hand to his suit's stomach Cathode can see the air escaping from between the fingers on his right hand. Even with his hand pressed firmly against his abdomen he can't make it airtight. The escaping air takes large stringy beads of blood with it. His hand slips slightly letting out a hard whine of air and floating blood particles. She forces her eyes to stay clear one last time.

No...

Lazy sees her face contort and tries to make his goofiest smile possible. Blood escapes from between his teeth as he coughs. Cathode weakly smiles back at him.

100%

The console chimes as the data file completes transferring to the other Superfluous.

"OK. It's sent."

Her voice is wavering as she speaks. The other Cathode responds.

"OK. Received."

Cathode opens her mouth as if to make a final speech but pauses. She unbuckles herself from the pilot seat and her body floats up slightly. She maneuvers herself over to the co-pilot seat and gently lowers herself onto the dash in front of Lazy's seat. She puts a foot on his knee to steady herself. He makes a pained face. She almost laughs. Her smile stretches harshly back across her face as she begins to cry. Cathode leans her head forward so she is pressed visor to visor with Lazy. She looks into his eyes with hazy vision. He smiles back at her. With her free right hand she reaches out to grab the throttle control. She says one last thing.

"Bye... Again."

She drops the throttle control down. She can see his mouth moving as if he's saying "Bye" back to her but she can't hear him. The control panel reads a decrease in throttle of .5%. The bomb lurches forward. Lazy wraps both of his hands around Cathode's left hand letting his wound expel his oxygen and blood freely. She puts her right hand on Lazy's visor as the bomb strikes the front of the cargo hold. Out of the corner of her eye Cathode can see a second white sun expanding toward her for the briefest of moments.

"Full popcorn."

She, Lazy and the Superfluous are consumed in pure white energy for the second and final time.

www.ingramcontent.com/pod-product-compliance
Lightning Source LLC
Chambersburg PA
CBHW070539310726
48982CB00010B/1410/J

* 9 7 9 8 9 8 6 7 9 8 6 3 9 *